*For Ciena and David, who sometimes think
I'm funny*

—S.P.

*For Micah and Molly, who only need me
half as much as I need them*

—J.P.

*For Alec and Jarrod, who are embarking on
their very own incredible voyage*

—B.A.

* * *

Copyright © 2019 Disney Enterprises, Inc.

All rights reserved. Published by Disney • Hyperion, an imprint of
Disney Book Group. No part of this book may be reproduced or
transmitted in any form or by any means, electronic or mechanical,
including photocopying, recording, or by any information storage
and retrieval system, without written permission from the publisher.
For information address Disney • Hyperion, 125 West End Avenue,
New York, New York 10023.

First Hardcover Edition, May 2019
First Paperback Edition, January 2020

1 3 5 7 9 10 8 6 4 2

FAC-025438-19347

Printed in the United States of America

ISBN 978-1-368-02395-5

Library of Congress Control Number: 2018953270

Designed by Gegham Vardanyan

Reinforced binding

Visit www.disneybooks.com

SUSTAINABLE
FORESTRY
INITIATIVE
Certified Chain of Custody
Promoting Sustainable Forestry
www.sfiprogram.org
SFI-01054
The SFI label applies to the text stock

SHIPWRECKERS!

THE CURSE OF THE CURSED TEMPLE OF CURSES

OR, WE NEARLY DIED. A LOT.

SCOTT PETERSON AND JOSHUA PRUETT

WITH ILLUSTRATIONS BY BRIAN AJHAR

Disney • HYPERION

Los Angeles • New York

"LIFE IS A SHIPWRECK,
BUT WE MUST NOT FORGET
TO SING IN THE LIFEBOATS."

—VOLTAIRE,
AS INTERPRETED BY PROFESSOR PETER GAY

"LIFEBOATS ARE FOR
LIGHTWEIGHTS!"

—CAPTAIN KEVIN ADVENTURESON,
AS INTERPRETED BY CAPTAIN KEVIN ADVENTURESON

PROLOGUE

THE TEMPLE ATE PEOPLE.

At least, that's what the stories said.

The man in the dark canvas duster coat and panama hat knew to be wary, but he wasn't scared. At least not yet. It was in his nature to take risks. That's where the adventure was. And a temple that was rumored to swallow the curious sounded like someplace he would find plenty of adventure.

The sky growled above him, lightning like electric tongues lashing at the world below.

The man watched the rain cover the temple in a cold, thin sheet of water and was more impressed than he thought he would be as the rocks in the temple wall slipped and parted and then fell back, revealing a hidden door and pathway down. Down into the belly of the beast.

The man adjusted his hat and stepped inside the tomb, where doom awaited him.

***

Hours later and miles downriver, the man in the canvas duster would be found by locals, bloodied and unconscious. The temple had spat him out, keeping one of his arms for its trouble. But clutched tightly in his remaining hand was a green jewel, hard-won and powerful beyond measure.

It would be many years before anyone would part him from it.

And many more before anyone would be foolish enough to set foot inside the cursed temple again.

FROM THE JOURNAL OF CAPTAIN
KEVIN ADVENTURESON
(YES, THAT IS MY REAL NAME, AS FAR AS YOU KNOW)

Dear (Hopefully) Awesome Reader,

Welcome to my journal of awesome adventure that's awesome!

Some people say adventure is what you make it.

No, it's not. That's stupid. That's like something a lazy PE teacher would say. (I probably don't need to name names. You already know exactly who I'm talking about. Mrs. Stalder-Burke. There, I said it.)

Look before you leap.

Another stupid saying that is stupid.

If you actually *looked* before you leapt, you'd never leap, and then where would we be? Nowhere, that's where. And that's not a place you want to be. Believe me. I know. I've been there.

Adventure is in my name, and I never look before I leap!

Hi.

My name is Captain Kevin Adventureson.

You've heard of me, I'm sure.

I'm very handsome. I'm also exciting. And wonderful. I'm pretty much the best.

I've been everywhere, done everything, and looked better than everyone else while doing it.

I am a hero, an adventurer, a thief (allegedly), and pretty much the coolest guy you'll ever meet or read about in a million years. My kindergarten teacher thought I was "very bright" and "going places"—and she was right!

You're very lucky.

Lucky because the story I'm about to share with you is all about me, Captain Kevin.

I do *so many* incredible things in what you're about to read. I can hardly believe it myself . . . and I was there.

For the record—and legal reasons I can't really get into—I should probably at least mention that this story also features a boy and a girl who, I'm sure, have names. But I can neither confirm nor deny the peril they were in, or all the times they very nearly died (none of which were my fault . . . well, except maybe that thing with the mummies).

Rest assured, we all got out alive and lived to tell the tale.

Unless we didn't, and I'm a ghost.

That would be *so cool.*

So, if you're curious about what it takes to become a Shipwrecker, like me, read on.

Feel free to skip the sections with the boy and girl and just read the parts that I'm in. They're easy to spot; they're all the good parts!

CHAPTER 1
DOWN WITH
THE SHIP

THE WHARF WAS ABLAZE with activity, like a birthday party on the surface of the sun: the heat was explosive, everyone was having a good time, and no one could stand in one place for more than three seconds.

Messengers raced by on mopeds delivering strange objects, clothes whipping in the wind as they rocketed past within mere inches of one another. Local merchants were hawking their wares in two, sometimes three different languages to customers who ran from one makeshift kiosk to the next like Olympic sprinters in a competition for the best deal. Mini-forklifts danced heavy loads from warehouse to boat, then returned for more crates, retrieving them from the large metal-roofed buildings that crouched low and hugged the riverside.

It was colorful and exciting, but Mike Gonzalez didn't notice any of it. Even with a front-row seat at the bustling docks of the second-largest river on Earth, Mike couldn't get his nose out of his book.

As the world barked and shouted nearby, Mike sat on a small crate under the hot Brazilian sun, leaning forward, elbows resting on his knees, hands positioned just so, keeping the book open wide enough to read, but not so wide as to break the spine.

The book was full of monsters and larger-than-life characters, and Mike had already read it three times. He turned the page and leaned down, causing his thick, shaggy black hair to fall into his eyes. He brushed it aside with the back of his hand, then shifted his body, readjusting his messenger bag.

Mike's bag was covered in patches that promised passports to imaginary places. Some of them were handmade, but all of them featured locations you could only travel to in books—mystical forests, ancient underwater civilizations, and deserted islands.

For Mike, real life was fine; books were better.

"Come on, Momo!" called a voice from the real world, threatening to pull Mike from the refuge of the printed page. It was his little sister, Dani.

"Please don't call me that," he said, without looking up. "At least not in public, okay?" Mike stayed focused on his book, scanning for the place where he'd left off.

"Check out this ship!" said Dani. "It's awesome."

"I'm sure it is," said Mike. "But it's a boat, not a ship. And you should probably get down."

"Get down from what?" asked Dani. "You're not even looking at me."

"I don't need to," said Mike. "I know you're doing something dangerous."

Mike finally put the book down and looked over at the tour boat Dani was playing on.

She scuttled up and down the broken mast, long dark hair bobbing behind her. She moved impossibly fast, all four feet of her, from her impish grin to her hand-me-down tennis shoes; she was fighting imaginary pirates with dragon heads from the sound of it.

"Come on, Momo," said Dani. "We're on vacation!"

It had only been one day, one jam-packed day, and already their trip was more than he could have expected. Rain forests. Wild animals. A zip line. A jeep tour. Cool new exotic foods. And all of it prepaid, prepackaged, safe, and disposable. Mike had to admit, at first, he'd been a bit nervous about such an ambitious family vacation, but so far it hadn't been too bad.

Then he took a good look at the boat, and his enthusiasm all but vanished.

The whole family was scheduled for a guided tour up the Amazon River, an afternoon among the animals, but the tug at the dock looked like something you'd see rotting on the bottom of the ocean. And for all Mike knew, maybe it had been.

It reminded him of an old wedding cake whose layers had been removed, or an old steamboat from a Mark Twain story that had been flattened and was pouting about it. It was a dinky boat doing a lousy impression of a *bigger* boat.

Mike thought everything about it seemed slapped together in a hurry, patched with duct tape and delusions of grandeur. There were pieces of old cabinets and bookshelves stitched together to make the walls of the craft's center hold; they were also combined with salvaged chunks of cars and parts of other boats. Even an old vending machine had been enlisted to hold up part of the roof; the device still held old pretzels, chips, and what appeared to be a live snake. The entire vessel seemed like it had been designed by a toddler using every crayon in the box—colorful and full of inspiration and enthusiasm, but very little forethought or consideration for engineering or safety.

The Amazon, on the other hand, looked formidable. It was wide and powerful and went on longer than Mike could imagine—over four thousand miles of snakes and jaguars and piranha, twisting and turning through six different countries. With its churning, roiling waters, it seemed like it had been built exclusively for thrill-seekers.

Mike was more of an armchair adventurer, someone who would rather sit in the comfort of his own home and read about other people's "derring-do." But he didn't consider himself a homebody; he had been on the baseball team. Once. And he wasn't a scaredy-cat; he just saw no reason to stick your neck out unnecessarily. At twelve years old, he had more than enough drama in his life without going out and looking for it.

Dani hung upside down from a beam, calling out to her brother.

"I think this is gonna be a great expedition, Momo!"

Mike stood up, moved his bookmark, and closed his book.

"I wish that were true, Dani," said Mike. "But there aren't any more great expeditions, at least not out there. But in here . . ."

He returned his book to his bag and retrieved a new one. The cover yelled out in loud colors: *Bermuda Betty and the Black Triangle of Doom*.

"In here," repeated Mike, patting the book, "all the thrills we could ever need. We can travel to the other side of the world, and never have to leave our seats to do it. All the benefits, and none of the customary bugs and dirt."

Mike brushed some mud off his shoe with the bottom of his other shoe.

"I like bugs," hollered Dani.

She climbed higher, silhouetted against the hot noonday sun.

"Come on down," said Mike, waving the book in the air like a doggie treat. "I brought this for you. It's the one where Betty disappears into the Bermuda Triangle."

"I love that one," said Dani. "But no thanks. This is better than reading *Bermuda Betty*. I'm *being* Bermuda Betty."

Dani was what Mike's parents would call "a handful," and what he would call "a pain in the butt." Yes, he loved her, and yes, most of the time he even liked her, but at eight years old (going on eighteen), she was like a magnet for trouble. No, that wasn't quite right. A magnet draws things to it. Dani actively sought trouble. A little bit like Bermuda Betty, the heroine of her favorite action-adventure book series, Dani could be reckless and impulsive, and she absolutely refused to look before she leapt.

"Dad!" Mike called, with the singsong cadence of old news in his voice. "Dani's up way too high. She's gonna get hurt. Like *broken leg, dent-in-the-side-of-the-head* hurt."

"In a minute," said Mike's dad, face and eyes glued to his phone.

"It's fine, love," said Mike's mom. "Try not to worry. You're twelve, not thirty-nine. Let us handle your sister. Enjoy your vacation!"

"Yeah," hollered Dani, swinging from the mast like a gymnast. "Let them worry about me!"

Mike and Dani's parents were standing on the small deck of the tour boat with the other adults on their trip, who were all on their phones, too: checking social media, taking selfies, or calling the office, some all at the same time.

Dani finally dropped down to the deck and ran over to the steering wheel, big and wooden, like something out of *Treasure Island*. She turned it one way, then the other. Mike could hear the rudders scraping the bottom of the river below. The boat's engines were already running.

"You probably shouldn't do that," Mike said.

Dani sauntered over to the side of the boat and leaned out toward her brother on the docks.

"Why are you still out there?" she asked. "Climb aboard. We're gonna go on a dangerous river journey into mystery!"

"I don't know about that, Dani . . ." said Mike.

Mike knew there were no more mysteries to uncover, no more treasures to find, only money to spend, selfies to take, and worthless souvenirs to bring home.

"Just do what I do," said Dani, still cheerful. "Pretend."

Mike laughed.

"Come on!" She held out her hand to him over the gap. The distance between the dock and ship was wider than he would've liked. It made him uncomfortable. The boat drifted back and forth against its moorings, creating a sizeable gap, then closing the distance again like a giant mouth.

"Be careful on the edge there, Dani," said Mike, putting the book in his bag and gripping the strap.

"It's fine," said Dani. "Jump."

Mike wasn't ready to jump.

Instead, he looked up past Dani and noticed a haphazardly drawn hand-painted sign hanging on the back of the hold: SHIPWRECKERS: TOURS AND ADVENTURES WITH THE INFAMOUS CAPTAIN KEVIN ADVENTURESON.

The guy describes himself as "infamous," and named his company after crashed boats? thought Mike.

"His last name can't really be Adventureson, can it?" he asked. "I mean, is that allowed? Sounds kind of—"

"Awesome!" replied Dani.

How did they even find this guy? And why is he thirty minutes late for his own tour?

"Come on, *mijo*," Mike's mom said, her attention focused on her phone. "You're not going to have any fun if you don't try. This could be exciting! Like in one of your books."

"Yeah, but in my books, we don't end up as fish food at the bottom of the river," mumbled Mike.

He gave another skeptical look at the lackluster boat and kicked it with his foot.

"Hey!" shouted a tall, rugged man who ran onto the docks toward Mike. He was sweating, out of breath, and, oddly, not wearing any pants. But before Mike could react, the bare-legged stranger ran up and kicked Mike in the leg.

"Ow!" shouted Mike, hopping on one foot. "You kicked me!"

"You kicked my ship," said the man. "I'm Captain Kevin!"

CHAPTER 2
SETTING SAIL . . . BUT WITHOUT SAILS

"**YOU CAN'T KICK ME!**"

Mike grabbed his leg. He wasn't quite sure of the legality of kicking a preteen member of your tour group, but he was pretty sure bodily harm didn't come as a fringe benefit with the tour package his parents had bought.

"Well, you can't kick my ship!" the captain spat back as he quickly went to untie one of the lines mooring the vessel to the dock.

"It's a tour boat, not a ship," said Mike.

"It's the *Roger Oberholtzer*—and you're rude!" said the captain, looking over his shoulder nervously. Back toward the wharf, there was a kind of buzzing sound, like a group of people yelling all at once.

"Your boat—"

"Ship."

"Is called *Roger Oberholtzer*?" asked Mike.

The captain pointed two thick fingers at Mike. "That's MISTER *Roger Oberholtzer* to you!"

"You're really our captain? Captain Kevin?" asked Mike.

"The infamous Captain Kevin Adventureson, in the flesh!" said Captain No Pants.

Mike seriously couldn't believe it.

"Where are your pants, Captain Kevin?"

"Where are your manners, young man?" shouted the captain. "You're officially my least favorite person. Now, hush and let the adults talk, hmmm?"

The captain glanced over his shoulder again, and Mike turned, too. A crowd of people had streamed onto the wharf and were making their way toward the boat. Mike had seen enough old movies to know the group looked and sounded just like an angry mob.

"Do those guys have pitchforks?" asked Mike, squinting.

"Not as far as you know," the captain replied. With that, he leapt onto the deck of his ship-boat and addressed the surprised tour group.

"Hello, lovely tour people who all paid up front. I am your captain, Captain Kevin Adventureson, the infamous Captain Kevin! And welcome to your Shipwreckers Adventure Tour! Danger guaranteed! I am wearing no pants. And we are leaving now!"

The group on the boat applauded, then dispersed to take a better look at the view beyond the railing.

Dani jumped down onto the docks beside her brother.

"He's so cool!" she said, squeezing Mike's arm.

"He kicked me, Dani."

"I know!" she squealed. Her face broke out in the biggest

smile Mike had ever seen, and she ran back onto the boat, darting from place to place.

"Can't say I've ever cared for dawdling on the docks," the captain said, glancing at Mike as he moved to the edge of the boat. "Too much *pier* pressure."

As Captain No Pants started to untie the *Roger Oberholtzer* from the dock's other moorings, Mike watched the cluster of shouting people getting closer and closer to them.

"Friends of yours?" asked Mike.

"Yes," said the captain. "Dear, dear friends. Come to see us off." He pointed to the line nearest Mike. "Now, stop standing there and help me."

Mike tried to untie the line.

"It's tight," said Mike.

The captain leapt back off the boat and crouched at Mike's side.

"That's the point, kid," said the captain. He smacked Mike's hands out of the way and untied it himself. "They only come two ways: *knotty* or nice."

Mike wasn't sure what was worse: the captain's bad puns or the captain himself.

Dani reappeared.

"What can I do?"

"Hoist the sails!" the captain cried. "You can be our *sails* manager."

Dani pirouetted like a ballerina, eager to do just that, before stopping in her tracks.

"This isn't a sailboat!" she protested.

"Ha! Just pulling your leg. *Schooner* or later I do it to everyone," the captain said.

"Really," Dani continued eagerly. "Can I help?"

"No," said the captain. "Not unless you can steer a ship."

Dani raced away across the boat and out of sight, spinning like a top. This did not bode well.

The captain looked back.

The mob was on the dock and running now, their angry shouts attracting the curious stares of messengers and merchants alike.

"We need to be gone," said the captain.

Mike looked at the captain's face and saw that his confident smile had dropped. Whatever this guy was running from was serious. Mike's stomach grumbled, which roughly translated to: *Yo, Mike. This is bad.*

Just then, one of the moorings snapped.

"Oh, good, the boat's already leaving," said the captain. "Wait. The boat's already leaving?!"

The boat was indeed drifting away without them.

"Who's driving the . . . ?" asked the captain. Then he and Mike saw Dani at the wheel, waving at them.

"Who's that kid?" asked the captain.

"My sister, Dani," said Mike. "You just made her sails manager."

"I like Dani," the captain said. "I don't much care for you."

"The feeling is mutual," said Mike.

There was a loud cry behind them. They both shot worried looks at the approaching mob, which didn't seem anything like the local crowd. At first, Mike thought they might be a group of angry tourists; but upon closer inspection, they looked more like cosplayers dressed as villainous comic book goons, sporting oddly shaped faces with menacing scowls, fedoras, and Bermuda button-up shirts, and wielding spears and pitchforks.

Mike looked at the boat and the rapidly growing distance between it and the dock.

"Come on, kid. If you're not gonna jump yourself, I'll have to do it for both of us." The captain grabbed Mike, and suddenly they were airborne, leaping for the deck of the ship.

The captain landed, rolled, and popped up with a little too much flair, arms extended and palms open. Mike, however, caught the lip of the deck with the tip of his shoe and tumbled forward, landing like a newborn giraffe, limbs flailing wildly. He hit the deck hard, hurting his arm and his leg—and his face.

"Ow," said Mike.

"Yeah, that's a real *hardship*," joked the captain.

Then Mike heard something whistling.

A spear flew by, striking inches from his head, and sinking its tip four inches into the vessel's top deck.

Mike's eyes almost popped out of his head.

He scrambled like a crab behind some boxes on the deck as the rest of the tour group gathered around to watch. Captain Kevin hid in the middle of them, keeping his head low.

Thup! Thup! Thup!

Three more spears struck the boat, the last one hitting the rope that held the SHIPWRECKERS sign. The heavy piece of wood dropped to the deck with a bang that momentarily startled the passengers.

Then they applauded.

Mike was stunned; they thought it was all part of the show. He risked a look back at the shore and was relieved to see that they'd put a safe distance between themselves and the captain's pursuers. Well, at least far enough that their spears would fall short, plunging harmlessly into the Amazon River, like butter knives dropping into dirty dishwater.

"Everybody wave goodbye to the beautiful people on the shore!" said the captain.

Everybody did as they were told, smiling and waving.

"Now everybody wave goodbye to the ugly people on the shore!"

The passengers laughed and waved as Mike nervously watched the angry mob glaring at the boat, and more specifically, at the captain, with murder in their eyes.

Mike's stomach knotted up. He hadn't come looking for adventure, but clearly it had come looking for him. This was going to be an interesting day. Maybe even one for the books.

CHAPTER 3
SHIP OF FOOLS!

THE *ROGER OBERHOLTZER* coughed its way down the river.

Dani thought it was cute, the way it chugged along like a little choo choo train. She leaned over the railing and looked across the brown waters of the Amazon toward the distant shore. A roof of leaves curved overhead like a natural archway, and all around her were the chirps and clicks and buzzing of the bugs and beasts in the rain forest.

But none of that was as cool . . . and wonderful . . . and amazing as Captain Kevin. In addition to his hat and faded T-shirt, he was now wearing a pair of shorts and an old life vest. Both his T-shirt and hat shouted the cool SHIPWRECKERS logo.

"Captain Kevin," Dani called, staring up at the tall man at the wheel. "Why is your company called Shipwreckers?"

"I'll tell you," he said with a smile and a wink. "But first . . ."

He leapt up on the railing to address all of his passengers, one hand held high over his head, waving like a movie star in a parade.

"Welcome, all, to the *Roger Oberholtzer* and, as I said, I am your captain, Captain Kevin. *The* Captain Kevin. You can clap now."

Everyone applauded. Dani clapped the hardest and the loudest. She glanced over to her brother. He looked like he was seasick. *Momo always did have a weak stomach*, thought Dani.

"You are all now my fellow Shipwreckers! Being a Shipwrecker is a part of a legacy, a long-heralded tradition from adventure stories of old!" The captain paused for effect, then leapt down to the deck to get up close and personal with his flock.

"From *Robinson Crusoe* to *Robinson Crusoe on Mars*, from *Tarzan* to the *Titanic*, from *Gulliver's Travels* to the *Swiss Family Robinson*, and all the others with Robinson in their name, so many great expeditions begin with a shipwreck!"

The captain opened his arms wide and spun in place, painting a picture with his movements.

"Shipwrecks are the catalyst to adventure, the dangerous door we pass through to travel to other worlds, the dark before the light, the bark before the bite, the tragedy before the triumph." The captain moved from tourist to tourist as he spoke, evangelizing as if he were speaking to each of them personally.

"That's what being Shipwreckers is all about. Also, it's catchy and it looks good on a T-shirt!"

They all applauded again.

"All right, *Roger*," the captain said as he leapt up to the bridge and patted the steering column. "Let's show these good people what the Amazon is all about."

"You talk to your ship?" Dani asked.

"You don't?" Captain Kevin replied.

"Who would ever put the very worst thing that could happen on their tour in the *name* of it?" Mike asked Dani.

"I think it's catchy," she said.

Dani gazed up at Captain Kevin, who was scratching his chest with one hand and drinking orange soda with the other. She noticed neither of his hands were on the wheel. *Impressive,* she thought.

He finished the last half of his soda in one gulp, crushed the can on his head, and tossed the trash at Mike.

"Souvenir," he said.

"Hey! You got orange soda on my shirt," cried Mike.

"Ooh! Thanks for reminding me!" said the captain.

He ran down belowdecks then came right back up with a flimsy cardboard box of Shipwreckers shirts and hats, announcing their outrageous prices and accepting cash from the tourists. Dani wanted two of everything.

"This is all damp," said Mike, examining the Shipwreckers merchandise.

"We're on the river, kid," laughed the captain. And everyone else laughed with him, Dani the loudest.

"And it smells," said Mike.

"That's the jungle!" said the captain.

"You already wore this," insisted Mike, holding up a shirt.

"It's got the adventure already baked in!" said the captain. He was glaring at Mike now. "That'll cost you extra!"

"'Adventure' or your sweat?"

"Same thing, kid," said the captain. "Same thing."

Dani took a whiff of the shirt herself. She'd never met

anyone like Captain Kevin in her entire life. It was like everyone else was black-and-white, like in those old movies Mike made her watch, and Captain Kevin Adventureson was full-color 3-D—big and loud and fantastic.

"What's with the life vest?" asked Mike, eyeing the captain's outfit. "Can't you swim?"

"Mike," cautioned Dani's mom, walking toward them. Dani knew the tone. It was a warning to "watch it." Dani watched her mom glare at Mike. Then she noticed Captain Kevin was glaring, too, curling his lip and flaring one nostril like a disapproving warthog.

"Please save all your questions till the end of the tour, when you're home and I don't have to look at you anymore."

Everyone laughed again. Everyone, that is, except Mike.

"And folks, if you get hungry or thirsty, this ship has everything you might want to eat or drink for very reasonable prices, including every vegetable but one. *Leeks*."

Dani laughed along with the other passengers. Then she spotted something adorable peeking through the green scenery.

"Ooh! Is that a monkey?" Dani cried, staring up as a furry creature swung through the foliage above their heads.

"Absolutely," Captain Kevin called out in a rich baritone. "On your left, you'll see a golden lion tamarin monkeying around way up in the trees. It may look like it has five legs, but that's just a tall *tail*."

Mike rolled his eyes. He did not seem as impressed as Dani was.

"Momo, we're on the Amazon!" she said. "The actual Am-a-zon! This is amazing!"

"*Amazonazing!*" the captain corrected.

"So, let's enjoy it," Dani said to Mike, lowering her voice.

"You're right, you're right," Mike conceded, looking at the vibrant jungle around them. "Even if this is all just a cheesy tourist excursion, it is a pretty amazing place."

The rest of the tour group, including Dani's parents, milled about the deck of the *Roger Oberholtzer*, chatting and taking photos, while Dani spun over to Captain Kevin, her new hero. She needed to know everything about him—and she needed to know it now.

"So, have you seen any dangerous animals? Did you ever get in a fight? Do you have any fake limbs? Have you always been a captain?"

"Of course. Dozens. None of your business. And since I was no older than you, but a great deal braver and more handsome," the captain answered.

Captain Kevin looked like an adult to Dani, but he acted more like a big kid. She wondered if they would be best friends, and quickly decided that they would be.

Dani asked the captain if she could have an orange soda, too.

"Sure, kid," said the captain. "Grab it from the anchor. I'll put it on your parents' tab."

"The anchor?" she asked, puzzled. The captain pointed to the chain hanging off the side of the boat and Dani ran to haul it up.

"Here," said Mike. "Let me help."

Dani yanked the chain away from Mike.

"I got it," she said. It bugged her how her brother never let her do anything herself. He was *waaay* too overprotective. It was like he thought Dani was going to break her arm or fall overboard just by touching something.

On the end of the chain, where an anchor should have been, was a dull red Igloo cooler.

"Keeps the sodas cold and the piranha distracted," Captain Kevin said.

Dani opened the dripping cooler and grabbed the soda, but struggled to pop the tab. The captain snatched it and popped it for her without even breaking a sweat. Dani grinned.

"I'll waive the uncorking fee," said the captain. "This time."

Dani downed half the soda in one gulp, her eyes never leaving the captain.

"Now, I will be steering us down a seldom-used tributary. You see, I've never been too fond of the *mainstream*," Captain Kevin joked to the passengers within earshot. "Besides, the river proper is just too trendy now, all hipsters and boring anthropologists. So, are we going off course? *Off course*, we are."

Everyone chuckled.

"Who's ready for the scariest, most dangerous part of our excursion yet?!"

"Scariest?" said Mike.

Mike pulled Dani close, but she pulled away.

"I'm ready," volunteered Dani. "What is it?"

The captain smiled and spread his arms wide.

"Shopping!"

CHAPTER 4
HOIST THOSE SALES

YES, THERE WAS a shopping mall on the Amazon River.

Well, not exactly, thought Mike. It was an open-air arrangement of tiny shops near the shore with a sunglasses kiosk, a snack stand, and even one of those curio shops full of odd objects from other parts of the world—you know, the type that seems to stay open in local malls no matter what else closes around it. This was nothing like the vibrant cultural exchange of the rest of the cities they'd passed through on their trip so far, full of warm people and colorful details. This was something completely different.

In a word, it was a tourist trap.

Okay, that was two words, but Mike knew one when he saw one. And seeing it plopped down there in the middle of the Amazon defied all logic, as well as everything Mike knew about that part of the world. Well, the parts he had read about in books anyway. It stood out like a sore thumb, or any painful appendage really, from the rest of the wild, natural world around it.

31

From the deck of the boat, Mike watched herds of tourists clamor for cheap trinkets and treasures he was pretty sure had been made in China, not Brazil or French Guiana . . . or even Ecuador, all the way at the other end of the river.

Captain Kevin docked the boat, barely five miles from where they had started, and like a pied piper of kitschy merchandise, he led his passengers off the *Roger Oberholtzer* and into the "unique local shopping opportunity."

To Mike, it wasn't just tacky; it was potentially dangerous. The crowds were too big, and there were too many places to get lost or lose a little sister in the overwhelming stampede of sales-hungry consumers.

As their parents disembarked, Mike hung back, grabbing Dani's hand.

"We'll catch up," he called. His mom and dad gave him a wave and they were off, already snapping pictures and posting them online.

"Hey," Dani protested. "Why can't we go?"

"It's all fake," he explained. "We're not missing anything."

"Come on, Momo," Dani sang, gesturing at the mall like a spokesmodel on TV. "They might have *boo*-oks!"

"I've got plenty," Mike said, patting his bag. "And besides, I just . . . I don't have a good feeling about this place. Feels a little shady."

"Yes," said Dani, still skeptical. "And . . . ?"

"And it's probably safer on the boat anyway."

"Ha! I knew it!" said Dani, pointing a finger at him. "You're trying to protect me! We're on vacation! There's nothing bad here, Momo!"

"You don't know that! You're still a kid. And when Mom and Dad aren't around, which they aren't, I'm in charge; and I am. I have seniority. You must respect the wisdom of my experience."

"You're twelve," said Dani.

"And a half," corrected Mike.

"I can't believe you think it's too dangerous to go *shopping*." Dani pouted.

"It's not that. *Pffff.* No," Mike lied, trying to backpedal. He knew she'd never stay if she thought protecting her was his only reason. "The real reason is, uh, this boat!"

"Ship," corrected Dani.

"Right. This ship, the *Roger Oberholtzer*—"

"MISTER *Roger Oberholtzer* to you . . ." corrected Dani.

"Yes, exactly," said Mike. "This boat is pretty darned cool, right? And we should, you know, investigate. Explore!"

"Seriously?" she stared at him through squinted eyes.

"Absolutely. Let's go!"

Dani shrugged and ran down the length of the boat with Mike trailing behind her. He sighed, feeling like he'd dodged a bullet. He could still hear Captain Kevin pitching to his tour group onshore.

"Take your time, folks," said the captain. "No rush. No rush at all. You may think that if you've seen one shopping center, you've seen *a mall*. Heh, heh. But that is not the case! Make sure you get enough for everyone back at home! Shop till you drop . . . your cash."

Once the last of the passengers had moved along, Captain Kevin ducked behind a thatched sunglasses hut. Then he ran, hunched over, toward the *Roger Oberholtzer*. With his eyes on the shoppers, he backed onto his ship, passing Mike and Dani without noticing them.

It was almost five minutes before Mike even registered that the boat was moving.

"Wait," said Mike. "We're moving?"

Panicked, Mike looked around the boat. No one was back yet.

He turned toward the shore, where his parents and the other tourists were getting smaller.

"No! Wait!" shouted Mike. "Wait!"

The boat was leaving.

Without their parents.

CHAPTER 5
ADVENTURE ALREADY IN PROGRESS: NO REFUNDS

MIKE WAS YELLING at the top of his lungs.

Captain Kevin—standing at the wheel of his ship, wind blowing in his hair—suddenly spun around to see two kids on the deck of his ship where there were supposed to be *no* kids on the deck of his ship—or anyone else.

"Wait! Wait!" Mike yelled. "Go back!"

"Bye, Mom and Dad!" Dani was at the railing, happily waving at the mainland as it drifted away. "Momo, was this part of keeping us safe?"

"No!" said Mike. He was officially freaking out. "I'm officially freaking out!"

"No!" the captain screamed, barreling toward them like a territorial rooster. "What are you two still doing here?" He pointed at Mike. "Especially you. You're not supposed to be here! You're supposed to be shopping!"

"Why aren't *you* back *there*?!" hollered Mike. "The tour

shouldn't be leaving without the tour group! That's, like, tour rule number one! Take us back!"

"Stop yelling!" barked Captain Kevin. "You're going to ruin my adventure!"

"What adventure?" asked Dani, her eyes widening.

"You're Dani, right?" asked the captain, suddenly shifting gears.

"Aye-aye." Dani saluted.

"Right, right," said the captain. "You're the one I like. My little copilot." He turned to Mike. "And if she's the one I like, that makes you—"

"Momo," Dani supplied.

"What kind of name is Momo?" asked the captain.

"It's not a name," Mike said. "And I asked you to stop calling me that, Dani. My name is Mike. Mike Gonzalez. Son of Abel and Christine Gonzalez, who you're going to take us back to immediately because you're responsible for your passengers—or at least you should be!"

Captain Kevin shook his head. "No, no, no. Number one, no one calls me responsible. How dare you? And another thing, this isn't even a tour, not really. The whole 'tour' thing is just what I tell people. It's what you might call a ruse, a facade, a distraction, a cover."

"For what?" asked Dani.

"Adventure!"

"Yay!" screamed Dani.

"Yup," said the captain. "You're the one I like."

"What kind of adventure?" asked Dani, her eyes wide as baseballs, hands grasped together in rapt anticipation.

"It's a story as old as time—and as wild as the sea. Um, or the river," Captain Kevin said. He put one hand on the wheel and one boot up on a barrel; he had to readjust twice in order to strike the exact kind of impressive pose he was after. "A story of men tampering with things they don't understand, of evil curses, and of temples that eat people. And treasure!"

"Ho boy," sighed Mike. He sat down on the deck and held his head. He couldn't believe any of this was happening.

Captain Kevin leapt off his perch and got very low to the ground, almost squatting so he could be closer to Dani's and Mike's faces.

"Many hundreds of years ago, a temple was built alongside the Amazon River," started Captain Kevin.

"Who built the temple?" asked Dani.

"Not important," said Captain Kevin. "What *is* important is that the rocks they used to build their temple came from hundreds of miles away."

"Like Stonehenge," said Mike.

"Like what henge?" said Captain Kevin. "Never mind. No talking."

He turned back to Dani.

"Legend says they made the rocks levitate using magic jewels, and that these jewels allowed them to move between dimensions, and travel instantly from one side of the globe to the other."

Mike perked up at this.

"Wait," said Mike. "You mean, like wormholes?"

"No," said Captain Kevin, wrinkling his nose like Mike had passed gas. "No worms. Yuck. I said no more questions."

"No," said Mike. "I mean, like doorways through space . . . wormholes—"

"Tut-tut-tut-tut." Captain Kevin cut him off, pinching Mike's lips shut with his fingers. Mike was too stunned to react. Had this guy really just clamped his mouth shut?

"As I was saying," the captain continued, "at first things were just great. But a few of them grew restless and greedy. They hoarded these magical jewels for themselves, and the more they collected, the more unearthly things they could do: Flying like birds. Passing through solid objects. Souls leaving their bodies. And eventually, raising the dead!"

Captain Kevin paused here for emphasis, getting serious.

"Stories say the gods grew furious with them and cursed the jewels. The power turned against them and their great temple came to life, devouring them for their transgressions, or whatever. They were never seen again."

Dani was staring, mouth agape, wide enough to catch flies.

"Some believe that inside that very temple sits a treasure unlike the world has ever known, protected with lethal booby traps and guarded by the mummies of the cursed corpses." Captain Kevin cleared his throat. "Now here's the good part. I have a plan."

"I feel better already," Mike said, sarcasm dripping from his words like drool.

"I have some friends who have a map that will lead us to the temple," Captain Kevin continued. "I'm headed to meet them now, and once I find that treasure, it will make me rich beyond my wildest dreams!"

"Oh, wow," said Dani. "Can we come?"

"No. Beyond the moral implications of proposing to steal rare artifacts that should belong to the local community, this is also insane," said Mike. "Great story, but utterly impossible."

"I scoff at impossible," said Captain Kevin. "Scoff!"

"It's ridiculous," Mike said. "There's no such thing as cursed mummies. There's no such thing as treasure. Not anymore. And there's no such thing as temples that eat people. I kind of wish there was, but there isn't."

"Here he goes," sighed Dani.

"Look," Mike continued, "if those kinds of things were real, we'd know by now. We'd have pictures of the Loch Ness monster on sonar. If Bigfoot was out there, he'd be tagged. In a world where you can pull out your phone and see yourself from a satellite camera in space, there are no real monsters or mysteries anymore."

"Your brother's a buzzkill," said Captain Kevin, pouting.

"If all this were a story, if this were a book or a comic, I'd have read it ten times already, and I'd be your biggest fan, asking for your signature!" Mike said.

"Signatures are free with purchase of a head shot," said Captain Kevin. "No selfies."

"How in the world can you expect us to believe that story?"

"That's a fair question," said Captain Kevin. He rubbed his chin, thinking, and appeared to make a decision. He lifted his baseball hat with one hand, and retrieved something from it with the other. Mike and Dani leaned in and Captain Kevin opened his hand, revealing a large green jewel.

"Whoa," said Dani.

Before they could get a good look, the captain returned the sparkling jewel to its hiding spot and pulled down on the brim of his hat.

"Is that . . ." started Mike.

"Yup," said the captain. "I . . . *borrowed* it from a friend. He claimed that it was the key to finding the rest of the treasure. Almost like a compass, or a magnet, drawn to the rest of the jewels."

"Like they're a family," Dani said in awe.

"I don't know about that," the captain chuckled. "I'm sure ninety-five percent of it is a lie, and that's being generous. But if that five percent is true, then that treasure exists. And with the map I'm about to acquire, I'm gonna find all of its brothers and sisters."

"Whoa," said Dani again.

Captain Kevin put his hands on his waist and stretched his back, cracking it like a stack of walnuts.

"Believe me, I don't like having you two here any more than you do, but if you can promise to keep quiet, I won't kick you overboard. As soon as we get the map, I'll bring you right back to your folks. This is just a little detour. Should be a few hours, tops. Deal?"

"Deal!" said Dani.

"What? This is still wrong," said Mike. "You abducted us. This is an abduction."

"*And* a treasure hunt!" said Captain Kevin. He hopped up and went back to the wheel. "It's a twofer!"

"Thank you, Momo," said Dani.

"You're welcome," said Mike. But then he thought about it. "Wait. Thanks for what?"

"For this adventure," said Dani, leaping all over the deck of the ship, the first kangaroo in the Amazon. "If we had gone ashore with Mom and Dad like I wanted to, we wouldn't be here right now! We're on a real adventure now, thanks to you!"

Dani hugged her brother hard, pushing the top of her head into Mike's cheek. Then she disengaged and bounced back to Captain Kevin. They high-fived, and Mike's heart sank.

Was she right? Was this really all his fault?

He quickly ran through the events of the day, processing what his sister had said.

Yes, thought Mike. *This is all my fault.*

Crud.

FROM THE JOURNAL OF CAPTAIN
KEVIN ADVENTURESON

So I stole the jewel, yes I did. But the guy deserved it.

And all that stuff about the mummies and the people-eating temples . . .

I made that up.

And the dimensions and magic powers and all that . . .

All fake.

But the rest of it was real.

As real as a three-dollar bill.

By the way, is anyone interested in buying some three-dollar bills?

(Note to self and future editor who will bask in my literary brilliance: cut that last line and replace it with another one of my hilarious jokes that people have come to know and love me for.)

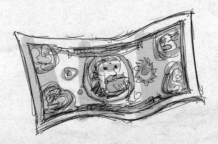

CHAPTER 6
MIKE TAKES CHARGE

MIKE AND DANI had been kidnapped.

Unintentionally, but kidnapped nonetheless. There just wasn't a nicer word for it.

Sure, Captain Kevin had promised to take them back to their parents, whatever that was worth. But as the captain droned on to Dani, lying back on one of the deck chairs, hands behind his head, cap over his eyes, Mike was more and more convinced that he couldn't just sit on his hands and do nothing.

But what could he do?

He knew he needed to have a backup plan, or five, just in case all this went belly-up.

Mike sat on the other side of the boat, swinging his book bag and chewing his thumbnail, a bad habit he'd started before he could even remember. For Mike, worrying was more akin to planning, or better yet, practicing for things that hadn't happened yet. He always ran through "what if" scenarios in his head, which theoretically saved him time and pain if and when they came to pass. But not everyone agreed with him.

His mother had called it "rehearsing for the worsing," but *worsing* wasn't a real word and he wasn't actively *looking* for worst-case scenarios; they just came to him easier than solutions did.

So Mike chewed his nail and thought, trying to block out the buzzing, bleating noise of Captain Kevin monologuing about his favorite subject: himself.

Slowly, ideas began to form in Mike's mind.

First, he thought he could grab Dani, jump in a rowboat, and paddle to safety. But when he clambered up and looked into the only rowboat the *Roger Oberholtzer* had, he discovered it had no bottom to step into. The boat looked like it'd been chewed on by something large and hungry and wasn't much more than an oblong wooden tutu. Mike imagined himself and Dani trying to escape in it and pictured them sinking to the bottom of the river, being devoured by a variety of horrid Amazon creatures, and leaving behind twisted skeletons to drift in the current for all eternity. Worst-case scenario.

He patted the rowboat with his palm.

"Thanks, but no thanks," said Mike. "Not worth the risk."

Still thinking, he wandered over to the boat's vending machine and quietly put in a few coins, trying not to wake the resident snake as he purchased an ancient-looking granola bar.

He moved to the stern, watching the wake of the motors spread to the far sides of the river. Mike eased open the wrapper and popped one end of the granola bar into his mouth.

It was as stale as Captain Kevin's jokes.

As he chewed, leaning against the rail with arms folded, Mike thought for a moment that maybe he and Dani could swim for it.

Mike crumpled up the granola bar's wrapper, stuffed it into his pocket, and tossed the remainder of the bar into the water.

There was a flurry of movement, like an explosion of popping popcorn in the water. He squinted and saw a school of razor-toothed fish leaping up out of the river toward the granola bar, sun bouncing off their scales and teeth.

Piranha!

Mike howled and scrambled away from the railing. He had forgotten about piranha, the most carnivorous fish in the Amazon.

All right then, thought Mike. *No swimming*.

Pacing the back of the boat, the meat of his fingertip still placed firmly against his teeth, Mike ran a few more scenarios for escape attempts, each of them theoretically thwarted horribly by fate or bad luck or the universe itself, which Mike was now convinced couldn't wait to see him and his little sister dead.

Mike felt confident this was true after discovering electric eels in the engine room, giant poisonous iguanas on the roof, and tarantulas, well, everywhere.

Every time Mike thought he had a way to get them off the boat, he was stopped in his tracks. They were all bad ideas. Terrible ideas. The type of embarrassing ideas that earn you nicknames at school like "Mayor McChump" and "The Bad Idea Bandito," or worse.

It wasn't a risk Mike felt like he could take.

In a book, Mike knew this challenge would be the "call to adventure," where the unsuspecting character is tasked with stepping up and becoming a hero. But sometimes the guy refuses the call.

Eventually, reluctantly, Mike conceded that maybe relying on the captain was their best course of action. Maybe it wouldn't *necessarily* mean certain doom. Perhaps it would even be a good idea to trust Captain Kevin. At least for the time being.

Resolved, Mike tossed the granola bar wrapper toward a greasy oil barrel that served as the ship's trash can, but missed. Mike went to pick it up, but Captain Kevin, apparently taking a break from talking about himself, was there first.

"Littering?" asked Captain Kevin. "On my ship?"

"Wh-what?" stammered Mike, bending over to pick it up. "No, see. Number one, this is not a ship. It's a boat . . ."

"Really?" said Captain Kevin. "Okay then." And with that, he neatly pushed Mike overboard.

CHAPTER 7
HIPPO CHOW

SUDDENLY, UNEXPECTEDLY, and without warning, Mike was in the Amazon River.

It was very wet.

Mike flailed, more from shock than anything else, then found his bearings and, a moment later, the surface of the water. He was swimming the best he could, but with the weight of his drenched clothes and book bag, and the speed of the boat ahead of him, Mike was almost out of breath and utterly exasperated.

"What! Why?" started Mike, but he couldn't finish the sentence. The only other words that sputtered out over the splashing of water and the drone of the engines were "repercussions" and "legal action."

"Right now, he's a little wet behind the ears," the captain joked to Dani, who had appeared at the rail, mouth open wide. "But he'll get used to it."

The water was warmer than Mike had expected, especially in the fading, pre-dusk sunlight. But the water was also darker than he'd thought it would be, and his imagination immediately went to work conjuring all manner of horrors waiting for him under the surface. Gators. Piranha. Jaguars with scuba gear. Heart racing, and trying desperately not to panic, Mike finally got one hand on the slow-moving *Roger Oberholtzer*.

"Help!" he called. "Hurry!"

Dani quickly kneeled down on the deck and reached out for her brother as he threw his book bag up onto the deck. It landed with a wet smack.

"Did you get it?" he asked.

"His books? Seriously?" Captain Kevin marveled.

"Tell me about it," Dani sighed.

"You're in deep water, young man," the captain said as he grabbed a particularly long oar from the deck to hold out to Mike. "But this'll do the trick . . . as soon as you admit that the *Roger Oberholtzer* is a ship."

"Boat!" hollered Mike, spitting river water.

"Ship!" said the captain.

"Momo!" said Dani.

"Fine," said Mike. "It's a ship."

"That's right," said Captain Kevin. "And which side of my ship did you fall off?"

"I was pushed off!"

"Which side?" sang Captain Kevin.

"Starboard side," said Mike. "Right side."

"Yes!" said the captain, offering the oar through a hole in the railing, then pulling it back like a shy dog's paw.

"No," the captain said, reconsidering. "Maybe! Hold on."

"What?" asked a frustrated Mike. He was getting tired.

The captain made an L with the pointer and thumb of each hand. He spoke quietly to himself, "Left, port. Right, starboard . . . okay!"

"Hey!" shouted Mike.

"Sorry, sorry," said Captain Kevin, squatting down on his haunches like an umpire to extend his paddle.

"Grab the oar," the captain said with a grin. "What are you *wading* for?"

"Lower," said Mike, coughing.

The captain leaned down farther, but he overshot the mark and bonked Mike on the head.

"Ow!" said Mike.

"Sorry!"

"You could stop the boat!" snapped Mike.

"Oh," said the captain. "Good idea." But as he got up, he glanced upriver and bit his lip.

"On second thought," said the captain, "I don't think you want me to do that."

"Why's that?" asked Dani.

"Why's that?!" hollered Mike.

Then Mike felt the waves shift, as though something else was moving in the water—something big.

"What was that?" asked Mike, panic in his voice.

"Nothing," said the captain, obviously lying. "A whole family of nothing!"

Mike craned his neck to look out across the river and spotted them.

All of them.

"Hippos!" shouted Dani, suddenly thrilled. "Hippos!"

"Oh, no," Mike moaned. As his head bobbed up and down over the surface of the water, he watched a pod of hippos—at least four or five of them, each the size of a compact car—head toward the boat. And Mike.

"Help!" said Mike.

"They're so cute," said Dani. "Cute and *really big*. Are hippos friendly?"

"Yes," said the captain, sticking his shoulder through a hole in the railing, extending the oar a little bit lower this time. But, of course, he misjudged the distance and hit Mike in the head again.

BONK.

"Ow," said Mike. "And no, Dani, hippos are not friendly. They're dangerous, and their eyesight is very poor. Especially at dusk, like right now-ish! They also shouldn't even be on this continent! They may have escaped from a zoo or something. Doesn't matter because they're here now! And that's bad!" He attempted a deep breath and gulped down some river water. He sputtered, then continued. "I've read that they can be very territorial and have mistaken humans for food!"

"What?" asked Dani, her excitement finally transforming into mild concern.

"No, they don't. They never do that," said Captain Kevin, reaching out with the oar again. "As far as you know."

BONK.

"Okay, okay, I've got this," said the captain. "Keep your eyes on me! Don't look at them, look at me!" There was something serious in the captain's tone this time. It was a side of him they hadn't seen.

Mike, of course, didn't listen to the captain's warning, and turned to see the massive jaws of a hippo, stretched impossibly wide and blocking out the fading sun. He ducked and moved his body just as the hippo took the oar out of the captain's hands and bit it clean in half. It glided off in the other direction.

"See? We're playing fetch. He's gonna bring that back," said the captain. "Maybe."

"Help!" screamed Mike.

Captain Kevin brought out a second oar, and Dani disappeared and returned with a third, holding it out toward her brother.

"Don't worry, we have so many paddles, it's *oar* inspiring," the captain joked as he held his paddle out. "My paddle or hers. It's an either *oar* situation."

"I want a refund!" screamed Mike.

"Adventure is nonrefundable," said Captain Kevin. "Just like real life!"

Mike could feel the water moving behind him, pushed by the other giant creatures headed in his direction. They were close and on their way to being much too close.

"Momo!" said Dani.

Mike took a deep breath and grabbed his sister's oar with both hands. Dani, both feet planted firmly, pulled hard on the paddle as Mike scrambled up and over the rail. He fell to the deck like a soaking wet bag of potatoes.

At that moment, it occurred to wet-bag-of-potatoes Mike that trusting Captain Kevin was probably going one oar too far. He lifted his head, squinting at the captain and his sister. If he wanted to make sure that he and Dani would survive this, he would need to be even more vigilant than usual.

Then he collapsed back onto the deck.

CHAPTER 8

IT TAKES A VILLAGE . . . TO HOUSE THIS MUCH SCUM

DANI WAS BUZZING.

She looked down at her brother, who was still trying to catch his breath on the deck. For a split second, she could acknowledge that, yes, he'd just had a near-death experience with a pod of hippos, and yes, he had probably almost drowned, and yes, he'd maybe probably very nearly died. But he hadn't! And there were hippos! Real-life hippos!

And now the captain was heading to shore, where they could hopefully have even more adventures. And maybe with more hippos!

They approached a dilapidated dock, where an emaciated man was slumped against one of the posts. But as they drew closer, Dani could see it wasn't a man at all—or at least, it wasn't a man *anymore*.

The human skeleton, wrapped in rags like a mummy, was tied awkwardly to one of the dock posts. It was shriveled and stiff, and wearing a colorful shirt and a straw hat, which made it kind of cute.

Dani saw Mike eye the mummy-guy and shudder a bit.

"Dani, I don't think that's a Halloween decoration," he said seriously.

"Cool," said Dani, her voice deep with macabre joy. Dani was still too young to think skulls and skeletons were anything *but* "cool."

Dani adjusted the SHIPWRECKERS ball cap the captain had given her. The hat was way too big, almost comically large on her head, its brim still flat and fresh out of the box. But she loved it.

With her new hat in place, Dani looked off the side of the boat and noticed that the captain had overshot the dock. They were floating right past the lounging skeleton.

"Sorry, *Roger*," the captain said.

He took a very long and very wide turn before heading back. The *Roger Oberholtzer* groaned with every shift of the engine and adjustment of its deep rudders. That combined with Captain Kevin apologizing to the boat over and over again reminded Dani of watching her uncle Oscar make a twelve-point turn with his prized convertible, agonizing and taking what seemed like hours.

"What's up, *Dock*?" the captain asked as his boots hit the wooden planks once they finally pulled in and disembarked.

Dani tromped across the short wooden dock, but then felt something yank on her arm. She turned around to see Mike, focused on the eyeless sockets of the skeleton guy.

"*Um* . . . maybe we should stay here," mumbled Mike,

more to the skeleton guy than Dani. "You know, on the boat. Where it's safe."

"Oh, yeah," she smirked. "You wanna stay here on the boat? Really? Because that worked out so well last time. . . ."

"Low blow," said Mike.

"Don't sweat it, kid," said the captain. "We're gonna meet my business associates, grab some grub, do what I do best, and then we get you back to your parents. Easy-peasy. As far as skeletons or mummies or whatever else is out there . . . you just stick close to me. I got this."

"Don't worry, big bro," said Dani. "I'll protect you."

Dani grabbed Mike by the hand, which he reluctantly accepted. Slowly but surely, they made their way across the short dock and into the jungle brush.

They took a path through a clearing and into more jungle. The day was still hot, and the early evening air was thick and wet, as if the sky were sweating. From time to time, Dani would catch a glimpse of a path beneath their feet, but it seemed to disappear and reappear at random. Dani imagined that maybe that was because the place they were headed was magical.

Eventually, they came to another clearing and something that looked a little bit like a city, or a garbage dump. Or both. It wasn't like any of the other bustling cities or beautiful villages they had encountered on their vacation before boarding Captain Kevin's boat. This one looked like it had been cobbled together by destructive visitors who had brought their junk and never left. Most of the buildings seemed slapped together using bits of strewn and discarded metal, or thrown together with old street signs and car parts. Donkeys and packhorses were tied to posts between motorcycles and SUVs up and down the street.

The place was dotted with people who looked to Dani like they were all characters in a Bermuda Betty adventure book, each of them with hidden agendas, dangerous desires, and tough-guy names. Most of them were missing limbs, or eyes, or both—and were scarred in strange and hideous ways. Some were bandaged or wearing layers of clothes like strange armor. More than a few had machetes the size of her arm; a few even sported nooses in search of a neck. One or two of them resembled aliens.

"Look at that guy!" exclaimed Dani. She pointed as a man with a head like a piñata strolled by. He was being followed, appropriately, by a shorter man with a baseball bat.

The captain told the kids to wait near the entrance to an alley while he went to talk to someone. Mike pulled Dani close and whispered in her ear, bursting her bubble.

"All right, Dani, if we can find a phone or a policeman, we can try to contact Mom and Dad. Or maybe another boat captain, who we can hire to take us back. If we hurry, we may be able to get back to them before dark."

Dani tried her best not to roll her eyes.

"But I don't want to leave yet, Momo."

"I do," said Mike. "And I know better."

"You're my brother, not my boss," Dani reminded him.

"Sometimes I'm both." Mike took a deep breath and stood up as straight as he could, sticking his chest out.

"What are you doing?" asked Dani. It looked to her like he was trying to muster up his courage. And failing.

"I'm going to get help. Stay here."

"Aren't you always telling *me* not to talk to strangers?" said Dani.

"Do as I say, not as I do," said Mike, parroting his parents. He walked up to the first person he saw. The heavyset man limped on a peg leg, scratching his oversized belly with a hooked hand. His beard tumbled down past his belt buckle, dirty and gnarled like a rat's nest.

Mike backed away.

"Okay, not that guy. He seemed really busy. Maybe this next one," Mike said, approaching a woman on the opposite side of the street. She was hunched over, long black hair completely covering her face and wearing a patchwork cloak draped over every inch of her body; well, every inch but her hands, which held a long, sharp knife that she constantly turned over and over.

Mike tiptoed away from the knife-wielding woman without saying a word.

"Chicken out much?" Dani whispered.

"Fine, fine," Mike said. "The next guy for sure."

Mike then marched up to a man wearing overalls. The man turned, his scarred, twisted face snapping and growling, startling Mike so badly that he stumbled backward and fell on his butt.

Mike stood and went to lean on Dani for support.

"Good one, bro," said Dani.

"See what happens when I stick my neck out?" asked Mike. "I almost get my head bitten off."

"Well, duh," Dani said, hands on her hips. "Not every risk

you take turns out perfectly. That's why they call it a risk. Then you try again."

Suddenly, the captain leapt in front of them.

"Hey!" yelled the captain.

"Aghhh!!!" cried Mike and Dani.

"Great news! I found the place where we're meeting my contacts!" The captain pulled Dani by the arm, and Dani grabbed hold of Mike as they weaved their way deeper into the village.

"It's a hole-in-the-wall taco place, and get this: it's the home of the world's hottest hot sauce! So hot, it could *kill* you! Come on!"

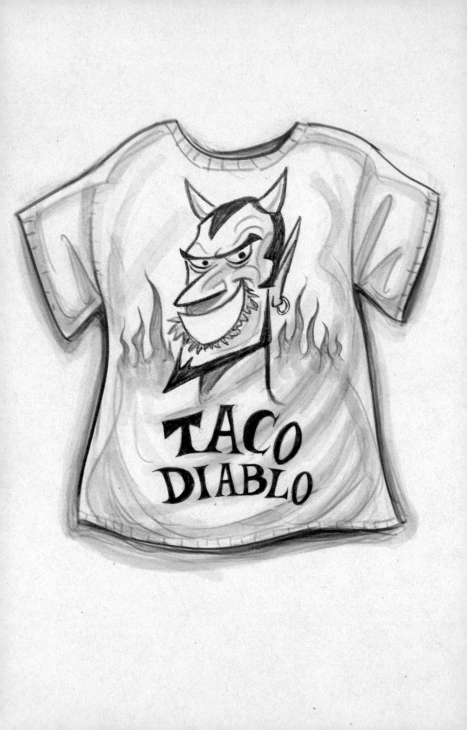

CHAPTER 9

TACO DIABLO: SAY GOODBYE TO YOUR MOUTH

THE DEVIL HAD A TACO for a mouth.

Mike wasn't sure what to make of the crudely drawn Taco Diablo logo, but it was clear that hot tacos and devils with wild eyes and sharp teeth were a major part of the restaurant's motif. Mike was confused as to why there was a traditional Mexican eatery in the middle of Brazil, but that was the least of his worries.

The captain had led Mike and Dani to the end of a dirt-lined street, then made a left turn into an alley that reeked of despair. That was where Taco Diablo sat, or more accurately, where there was a small opening in the crumbling brick; it was a literal hole in the wall, which you had to climb through to get inside.

Crawling through the mud-brick wall was like traveling to another world entirely.

The "restaurant" was dark, lit by candlelight, and Mike had to squint to see more than a few feet in front of him. While it seemed to be a large place, the sheer number of makeshift tables and patrons made it feel very cramped and claustrophobic. You couldn't walk more than two feet before bumping into someone—and these were not people you wanted to bump into.

Shadows played games with the customers' features, and the hairs on Mike's neck stood up, stiff as number two pencils. He usually prided himself on not judging a book by its cover, but there were some gnarly covers in this place. Yes, it was clear to Mike that this place attracted a very particular kind of clientele, not the friendly local folks they'd seen along the river.

And from the stares he was receiving, Mike figured kids were not usually welcomed here. Most of these folks looked like the last kid they'd seen was the one they'd eaten for breakfast.

Glancing up, Mike saw cheesy papier-mâché piñatas hanging down from the ceiling. But all their heads had been replaced with skulls—real or fake, he couldn't tell.

Captain Kevin led them back to a table that was made of apple crates and lit by a sputtering candle. A waitress with sharp eyes and long blond hair set out three waters for them. Tall, composed, and confident, she seemed out of place in this dive.

The waitress looked Dani and Mike over before handing them menus and saying she would be right back.

"Cool place, huh?" asked the captain.

"Yeah!" said Dani.

"My associates are on their way, so we should eat while we wait," he said. "I'm gonna do the Taco Diablo challenge!" He eagerly pointed to the wall.

Mike squinted at a bulletin board sporting a faded T-shirt

with the Taco Diablo logo on it, as well as photos of men who seemed to be in agony. At the top of the board were the words HALL OF FAME.

Apparently, these men had taken the Taco Diablo challenge and lived long enough to get their picture taken. But only just barely, judging by their pained expressions.

"I thought you were in some three-alarm-fire rush to get to your treasure," Mike said. "So much so that you couldn't possibly take us back to our parents. But now you're going to sit and take on a taco challenge?"

"Okay, one: I don't like your tone," the captain fired off. "Two: I just told you, we have to wait here anyway for my contacts to show up, so sit down and be quiet. And three: that T-shirt is mine!"

He grabbed the menu and unfolded it. And unfolded it again. It was ridiculously huge, like one of those sun visors you put in the front of your car on a hot day. Maybe larger. Mike was surprised to find that the back of it featured a crossword, a word game, and a map-styled connect-the-dots, like a big activity place mat for kids. It seemed weird for such a rough place.

The captain pointed to a highlighted section of the menu.

"Read it, read it," he said, evidently too excited to do it himself.

"It says to win the challenge, all you have to do is eat one taco . . ." Dani started.

"One taco! I got this," Captain Kevin said.

"Let's see," continued Dani. " 'Special brand Taco Diablo hot sauce—so hot it will kill you'—Ah, if you survive the five-minute afterburn without drinking anything, you get the

T-shirt. And your picture on the wall. And then there's lots of cute little skulls. Looks like their hot sauce is pretty hot."

"I want that T-shirt," growled Captain Kevin. "I love free stuff."

"There's a health warning here, too," said Dani. "It says—"

"Don't worry about that," said the captain, cutting her off. "I've done food challenges all over the world! This is going to be a walk in a park of tacos! Anyway, order what you want," the captain said generously. "Your parents are paying. Or at least, they will be eventually."

The waitress reappeared. Mike ordered a burrito (the menu implied that it would be as big as his head), Dani asked for some taquitos and a quesadilla (some days it seemed like all she ever ate was cheese), and the captain couldn't wait to get his Taco Diablo challenge.

The waitress stopped writing on her pad and stared at the captain, evaluating him.

"I don't think so," she said, looking from the captain to Mike and Dani, then back at the captain. "It's really hot."

"How hot?" asked the captain.

"Really hot," said the waitress. "Last guy had to be carried off in a stretcher and get a mouth transplant."

"Really?" asked Dani.

"No," said the waitress, smiling at Dani. "But that would pretty wild, right?"

Dani laughed. "I wanna see that."

The captain cleared his throat.

"One Taco Diablo challenge, por favor," he said, projecting his voice so most of the restaurant could hear him.

The waitress sighed.

"Are you clear on the rules?" she asked. "And the five-minute afterburn and—"

Captain Kevin didn't let her finish. "I got this."

The waitress stared for a beat longer, then left, taking the menus with her.

"So," Mike asked, "who are these people we're meeting?" He hated not knowing what was coming next—in life, but especially in his present circumstances.

"Just some friends," said Captain Kevin, gazing longingly at the shirt on the wall.

"Friends?" said Mike. "So, you know them pretty well?"

"Nope. Never met 'em," said the captain. "I like friends I've never met. I kind of wish I'd never met you. . . ."

"But—" started Mike.

"Look, kid," the captain interrupted. "I'm going to make a small business transaction with some new pals, win a free T-shirt, and then we'll be back on the ship and you'll be out of my hair! Relax and try to enjoy your vacation."

"Yeah, Momo," said Dani. "Try and relax."

"Yeah, Momo," repeated Captain Kevin.

"Please don't call me that," said Mike, shaking his head and closing his eyes.

"What's the big deal?" asked the captain. "*She* calls you Momo, doesn't she?"

Mike sighed. "When Dani was small, she couldn't really say my name," he explained. "Momo was all she could get out. And it stuck."

"Adorable," said Captain Kevin.

The waitress returned with the kids' food and set it down. In her other hand was a plastic basket with one taco covered in bright red hot sauce. She dropped the taco in front of the captain, then set a large glass bottle of the Taco Diablo hot sauce on the table.

"In case you want more, tough guy," said the waitress. Then she left.

Mike leaned in to get a closer look at the captain's meal. The taco seemed more hot sauce than actual taco. It was soaked in the stuff, and the smell made Mike's eyes water.

Captain Kevin took a deep breath, cocked his head to one side, and rolled his fingers in the air.

"Taco-eating position assumed," said the captain. "Now watch me teach this taco who's boss!"

Gently placing his thumb and fingers over the taco, he squeezed, lifting it from the basket.

"Ooh," said the captain. "Actually stings my fingers a little. Ha ha. Wow. Ouch."

Mike instinctively scooted back from the table a bit. Dani ate her quesadilla but kept her attention fixed on Captain Kevin.

The captain bit into the taco, hot sauce leaking out from all sides.

"Oh, sweet," said Dani, mouth full of quesadilla. "It looks like it's bleeding. Doesn't it look like it's bleeding?"

The captain smiled and chewed his bite.

"Not bad," said the captain, his mouth now full. "Not bad. I, uh, can't feel my tongue. Ha ha."

His cheeks were getting red. Sweat pooled on his forehead, and his eyes started watering.

"You okay?" asked Mike.

"Oh, yeah," said the captain. "Oh, yeah, definitely."

But Mike could tell he really wasn't okay. He wouldn't have said it out loud, but it was a little refreshing to see the captain this uncomfortable.

"Go, Captain, go!" said Dani.

"I'm going," said the captain, trying to rally.

Captain Kevin closed his eyes, then went to town on the taco, gobbling it up in three bites.

Dani cheered as the captain chewed. It looked like he was eating glass.

"Oh, boy," said the captain. He tried to open his eyes, but couldn't for more than a few blinks.

"It's pretty hot, eh?" asked Mike, as he purposely took a long, cold drink of water.

"Yeah. How long is that afterburn?" asked the captain, putting both hot sauce—covered hands on his glass of water. The captain's shirt was soaked clean through with sweat now. Something dripped from his nose to the table.

"You okay?" asked Dani.

"Yeah, yeah," said the captain, exhaling. "Kinda seems like it's eating me alive from the inside! Not a great feeling! You guys know how to tell if you're having a heart attack or not? What day is it? Is the room spinning? I can't feel my mouth at all. Do I still have one? Man, this is really not worth a T-shirt. I wonder if they'll bury me in it."

Mike could hardly keep from laughing out loud. He couldn't believe the captain had willingly done this to himself.

"Are you guys still there? Dani? Momo?" called the captain. "If only I could see . . ."

The captain lifted his hands to his eyes.

"Stop!" yelled Mike, snapping out of his amusement. "Your hands are covered in hot sauce!"

It was too late. The captain had shoved his fingers—still covered in the Taco Diablo hot sauce—into his eyes and rubbed them. Hard.

The captain screamed.

Everyone in the place turned to see the two kids trying to restrain the captain as he bucked and kicked and jumped, compensating for the pain in his eyes by moving every other part of his body.

"Oh, that was a mistake," said the captain. "Agghhh!! I'm blind and it hurts! Those are two terrible things! Oh, my face! Do I still get my T-shirt?!!"

Mike jumped into survival mode. "We gotta get you out of here," he said. "And get to a doctor."

"No, get me to my ship," countered the captain. "We'll go somewhere that I can get an eye transplant, and then I can die peacefully. Time to leave! Just one quick sip . . ."

The captain threw the contents from what he thought was his cup into his face, but it was actually the hot sauce bottle.

"That's not water!" said Mike.

The captain spat and sprayed the hot sauce all over the table.

"That's not water!" the captain repeated. "Oh, God, I'm dying. But very slowly! Where's my T-shirt?"

"Come on," said Mike, leading Dani and the blind captain away from the table. "Let's get back to the boat."

"Not yet, Governor," they heard someone from behind them say. Whoever was speaking sounded like a British nobleman with a terrible head cold. "We've only just arrived, haven't we?"

Mike turned to see a tall man in a white suit and wearing an eye patch standing beside a large, muscle-bound football player of a man covered in tattoos. The man with the tattoos was humming sweetly to himself.

"Captain Kevin, I presume," said the tall man. "Let's break bread together, shall we? There's so much to discuss. Sit down."

Mike could tell from his tone that this was not a request.

FROM THE JOURNAL OF CAPTAIN
KEVIN ADVENTURESON

Never trust anyone.

That's my motto as an adventurer and a Shipwrecker.

Well, that, and "Never go to bed angry or underwater."

But first and foremost, it's never trust anyone. Women. But also men. And kids, too, while we're listing things.

I'm not talking about the brother and sister duo who stowed away on my vessel to go adventuring with their hero. Who can blame them for that? No, those kids are, at most, a distraction, used to draw the attention of a hungry jaguar. (I always say, I don't have to run faster than the jaguar, I just have to run faster than the kids.)

No, when I say "never trust anyone," I'm talking about the people I have to deal with in my adventuring lifestyle. The smugglers. The barkeeps. The swashbucklers and mercenaries who start out in awe of my abilities, knowledge, and handsome allure, but slowly grow sour. A man can only have so many successes before admiration turns to jealousy.

Never trust anyone.

That's why I'm always on my toes, always keeping my wits about me, always ready for the other shoe to drop.

Even if that shoe is actually an anvil shoved into a size fourteen steel-toed boot.

CHAPTER 10
WITH FRIENDS LIKE THESE . . . RUN!

THERE WAS SOMETHING wrong with Captain Kevin's friends.

As soon as the two men appeared, the captain tried to act like he wasn't on fire from the inside out. With the hot sauce covering his face and eyes (and mouth and hands), it looked like he was bleeding from every orifice. Still, he was attempting to play it cool, like a zombie who didn't want you to know he was undead.

"Oh, hey," said the captain. "There you two are. You're right there. Right now. You're right on time."

The waitress reappeared and ushered them to a larger table. Mike thought he saw her share a brief look with the tall man, but he couldn't be sure.

"Can we get some water?" asked the captain. "Bring all the water. Bring a camel!"

They all sat in silence for a bit until the captain managed to cough his way through the introductions. The tall British man in the white suit and the eye patch called himself

Vincent. The strong guy was named Rube. Mike noticed that all his tattoos featured pugs making adorable faces. He spoke in a sweet tenor tone that had a singsong quality and there was a peppermint-candy smell on his breath.

"You smell like Santa Claus," said Dani.

"Thanks, love," said Rube.

"Well, this is a right awful place," said Vincent, making a point not to touch anything.

"Why do you always have to be so mean?" his burly companion asked.

"I'm not being mean," said Vincent. "I'm just being honest, mate."

"We talked about this," said Rube. "It makes me very uncomfortable."

"Well, I can't rightly help that," said Vincent. "This place is disgusting. That's as plain as the nose on your face. Even plainer than the one on this bloke's face . . ."

Vincent indicated the captain's nose.

"Certainly substantial, isn't it?" said Vincent. "It's right huge."

Mike laughed, then covered his mouth. He hadn't noticed before. But Captain Kevin's nose was pretty big.

"That's not very nice, either," Rube admonished. "Besides, you're way off. I would have said something about his ears before I said word one about his nose."

"Well, yes," said Vincent. "That goes without saying."

"Good point," said Mike. Maybe these guys weren't so bad after all.

"Hey," said the captain, the taco sauce turning his face pinker and pinker like an uncooked ham, "no teaming up."

"He's right," added Dani. "No fair."

Vincent squinted his one eye at the captain, sizing him up. "When I look at you, Captain Kevin," he said, "all I see are dollar signs. Oh, and that huge nose, of course. But that brings us to why we're all here today . . . well, all of us except for you two fine young people."

"Uhhh, they're related. To me. My relations," coughed the captain, his eyes closed in pain. "My niece and my nephew."

"Really?" asked Rube.

"Yup," said Dani. "He's my uncle Captain Kevin."

"Indeed," said Vincent. "Well, perhaps they'd like to run along like good little urchins while we conduct a little business . . . ?"

"We're gonna stay," said Dani.

Mike started to correct her, then stopped. Something was off about all of this, but Dani's instincts seemed right; going off alone was worse than keeping close to Captain Kevin. Or at least so he hoped.

Vincent curled his lip a bit. "Well, then, Captain Kevin. I believe we are ready to come to terms. If you have acquired the jewel we discussed?"

The captain hesitated, then pulled the green jewel out from under his ball cap and laid it on the table. Mike finally got a closer look. It shone like broken bottle glass—pretty and strangely hypnotic. Mike couldn't help staring.

"Yup, this is it," Captain Kevin said. "The jewel. The key

to the temple. You're not getting in without this. Does anyone else feel like they're melting?"

Vincent reached for the gem, but the captain, moving almost imperceptibly fast, yanked it back and slipped it back under his cap.

"Careful there," said Rube. "No funny business."

"Don't worry," said Captain Kevin, tears still streaming down his face. "Everything is fine! No funny business here!"

"Yeah, he tries constantly, but he's rarely funny," Mike confirmed.

"Do be careful," said Vincent. "The stories tell of a curse on that jewel. And of its incredible powers. I suggest we tread cautiously, hmmm?"

"Oh, yeah. Whatever," said the captain.

"So, how'd you get your eye patch?" Dani asked Vincent conversationally.

"It's a secret," said Vincent.

"Pirates? Wild baboon? Running with scissors?" Dani guessed.

The Englishman ignored her, staring instead at the captain, whose head now wobbled around like a bobblehead.

"You have the map?" the captain cried through gritted teeth.

"Are you okay?" asked Vincent finally. "You don't look well."

The captain tried to smile, but his tongue slipped out and hot sauce dripped down his chin.

"I'm peachy!" the captain replied.

Vincent exchanged a look with Rube. Then the tattooed man pulled out an old map and placed it on the table. The captain leaned forward. He tried to pry his eyes open wider to examine the piece of parchment, dripping hot sauce on the map.

"My word, man," said Vincent. "Are you leaking?"

"My bad," said the captain. "But from what I can see, this looks good."

"And you have a boat?" asked Vincent.

"A ship!" corrected the captain.

"Of course," said Vincent.

Suddenly, the captain let out a little gasp and started weeping. He coughed, attempting to compose himself.

"Then, then I guess we, we have a deal," sniffled the captain.

"Are you crying?" asked Rube.

"No," said the captain. "I'm so happy! And I might be dying!"

"He means he's so excited about the quest," said Mike, doing his best to cover. He wanted to finish the transaction and get the captain out of there. "In fact, I'm anxious to get started, aren't you, Dani?" He raised his eyebrows at her and she nodded.

"I sure am!"

As Mike moved to get up, Rube put a thick hand on his shoulder and pushed him back down.

"What's the rush?" asked Vincent. "Maybe we should get to know each other a bit better before we set sail, hmmm? Maybe take another look at that jewel of yours. . . ."

Mike looked back to the hole in the wall where they had entered just as three large men in rough outfits came through.

He could have sworn he saw one of them nod at Rube. He didn't trust the captain's "friends," and his gut told him that they needed to get out of there as soon as possible.

Mike tried to signal Captain Kevin, first motioning with his head, then winking his eye, and finally jerking his thumb toward the door. But the captain was well on his way to total blindness and saw none of it. Mike would have to be more direct.

"What do you think, Captain, er, Uncle? Uncle Captain?" said Mike. "Time to leave. It's getting late for us kids . . ."

"We're good," said the captain. "Let's order some more food. And water. Definitely some water. Water, waitress? Water!"

The waitress reappeared, and Rube and Vincent ordered the Nachos de Muertos.

"Uncle," Mike tried again.

The captain shushed him. "Don't ruin this for me," he whispered.

"But Uncle," said Mike. "We need to leave *now*." He saw Rube pull a large baton from under the table. Mike glanced around the room once more. Every single person in the restaurant was looking their way now.

Starting to sweat, Mike turned back to Rube. The tattooed man smiled at him.

"Don't worry, kid," said Rube. "This will all be over soon."

Suddenly, things moved very quickly. Singing what sounded like a lullaby, Rube lifted his weapon and lunged for the captain. But before he could connect, Dani leapt over the table and bit his tattoo-covered arm.

Rube screamed, shaking Dani loose and knocking the table over. The plates, map, and candle went flying into another group of patrons, who leapt to their feet, furious.

The entire room erupted in chaos as a brawl broke out. But even in the mayhem, Mike could see that several burly customers were headed straight for their table. The captain remained seated, crying with his eyes closed as Vincent dove at him.

"I just wanted that T-shirt," sobbed the captain.

Mike quickly pulled the captain to the ground—just out of Vincent's grasp—seconds before four more men dove into the fray. It seemed Vincent and Rube weren't the only ones after Captain Kevin.

"Grab the map!" the captain shouted.

But instead, Mike grabbed Dani by the seat of her pants and pushed her under the nearest table; for once in his life, he didn't think, he acted.

"Dani, keep moving!" cried Mike. Instead, she pushed past Mike to pull the captain along with them. They scrambled from table to table, trying to make their way to the exit hole in the wall.

The captain crawled on his hands and knees like a baby, fingers sweeping the floor, blindly in search of the map. And in a bizarre stroke of luck, he found it. But in more typical Captain Kevin fashion, he held it a little too close to a fallen candle. The whole thing caught fire.

"Whoops."

A few tables away, the other patrons who'd pig-piled on Rube and Vincent finally regrouped and noticed that they'd lost their quarry.

"Not us!" shouted Vincent. "Get *them*!"

Mike looked around, desperate for another exit strategy. But all he could see were brawling customers and tables and chairs flying around the room.

Then Mike was hoisted into the air.

Rube held him up like a doll, still singing his ballad.

Thinking fast, Mike grabbed one of the skull piñatas from the ceiling and slammed it down over Rube's head.

The brute dropped Mike. He scrambled over to his sister and the captain, who'd made it to the hole in the wall.

They were about to leap through when a figure in a white suit blocked their path.

Vincent.

"Leaving so soon?" he asked.

Grabbing a bottle of hot sauce off a nearby table, Dani splashed it across Vincent's face, most of the red stuff landing in his good eye.

Vincent screamed and fell back, clawing at his burning eye socket. Seizing his moment, Mike pushed the captain through the hole. He reached to grab Dani, but Rube got to her first. Still clutching the bottle, she threw what remained of the hot sauce into his eyes, too.

Rube cried out and dropped Dani into her brother's arms. They dove through the hole and landed on the captain outside the restaurant.

Night had fallen while they'd been in the Taco Diablo, and the village was dark and foreboding. But right then Mike was more worried about what was behind them than what might be waiting in the darkness.

"Move!" he yelled.

They all jumped to their feet, and the captain ran straight into a wall.

"Ow," said the captain. "Little help."

"Come on!" said Mike. Each took one of the captain's arms and dragged him away.

"What about my T-shirt?" asked the captain.

Behind them, the hole in the wall of the Taco Diablo spat men into the alley like rats escaping a sinking ship, all of them hot on Captain Kevin's tail.

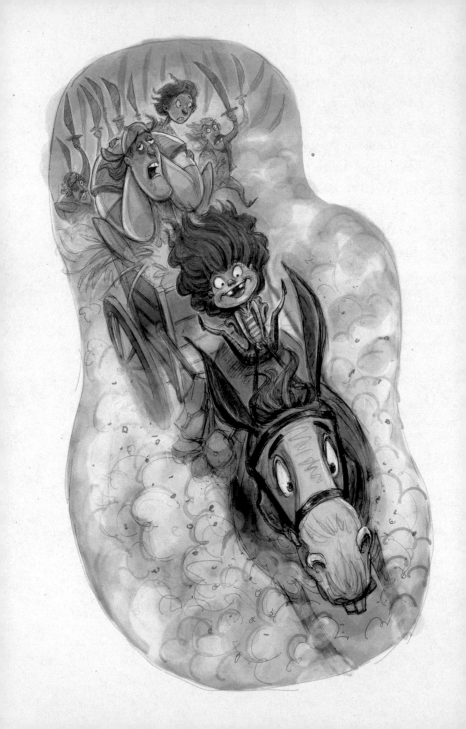

CHAPTER 11
TACOS GIVE ME THE RUNS

MIKE WAS PRETTY SURE they were gonna die. But it didn't stop him from running.

And trying to run while dragging the limp, blubbering captain was almost impossible. They'd advance a half block or so, then have to stop, pick him up off the ground, and start again. It felt like they were babysitting a toddler.

Mike turned back after a few stops and was startled to see the troll-ish folks from the Taco Diablo charging out into the street.

"This way," said Dani. She led them into an alley. Then she darted around a corner and ducked.

A beat later, she leapt up, guided them to another spot, and ducked again.

Up and down, up and down Dani and Mike bobbed; it was a bit like playing a video game. Dani focused on getting them from one hidey-hole to the next. Mike was impressed, though there wasn't much time to express it.

But more to the point, he knew they couldn't keep this up forever.

They exited another alley and spotted a donkey cart ahead. Mike and his sister dragged the captain behind it just as three goons ran by.

"I get it now," said the captain, whispering. He seemed delirious. "Momo. Take away the last *O* and your name is Mom! Ha! I can't feel my insides!" The captain pounded the ground, startling the donkey. It hurried away with the cart, exposing them to their pursuers.

"Oh, no," Mike muttered. As if on cue, he heard someone with a deep voice yell. Turning, he saw two guys running their way, flaming torches held over their heads.

"I've got another idea!" Dani cried, grabbing his arm. "Come on!" She sprinted after the donkey, while Mike pushed the captain after her. They dove onto the moving cart, the captain falling flat on his face.

"Ow," said the captain. "There's a splinter in my ear."

Mike risked another look back and saw that they were leaving the thugs in the dust.

"Yes!" he said, with his fist raised in the air.

They shot down the town's main street—if you could call it a street. But the cart began to slow. Mike saw that the donkey did not seem as committed to running as it once was.

The Taco Diablo men, however, were gaining on them, apparently *very* committed—to running after them.

"Dani," said Mike. "What do we do now?"

"Don't worry," she replied, scrambling to the front of the cart and leaping onto the back of the donkey.

"Awww," she sighed, fawning over the ugly miniature non-horse. "You're so cute!"

"Dani!" yelled Mike.

"Oh, right." Dani kicked her heels—gently, yet firmly—into the sides of the donkey. "Giddyup, horsey!" she cried. The donkey took off like a shot into the night, propelling Mike back onto the rough flooring of the cart.

They sped through the town again—fast and out of control. The donkey seemed to have its motivation back, but no sense of direction whatsoever. And Dani couldn't really steer it.

The kids, at this point, were going around in circles just as the thugs finally caught up. They took swipes at the cart as it passed.

Things were going from bad to worse, and from worse to *How the heck did I end up here, and where's my mom?* Mike knew they had to get the moaning captain back to the *Roger Oberholtzer*. But the crowd of ruffians was gathering . . . and growing.

A whole group of Taco Diablo patrons swarmed the cart, a handful of them climbing onto the back and reaching for the captain.

"Faster!" Mike yelled.

Dani urged the little donkey to keep moving. Using the ropes from the cart as makeshift reins, she directed it toward the clearing at the edge of the town's borders.

"Good horsey!" yelled Dani.

Meanwhile, the roughneck closest to the captain grabbed his ball cap. Mike lunged for it, but the goons on the cart played keep-away, passing the cap among themselves.

The cart hit a bump, sending two of the troublemakers tumbling off the back. That gave Mike an idea. As two more hoodlums tried to pull the captain down and off, Mike dropped down and rolled into their legs. (It was a move he'd learned from fighting with Dani over the TV remote.) They toppled to the floor of the cart. Mike quickly jumped up onto the captain's shoulders, snatching the captain's hat and the jewel inside it from midair as it was being tossed about.

His victory was short-lived, however, as another long-limbed ne'er-do-well snatched the hat back.

"Who's that?" Captain Kevin cried, flailing blindly. He smacked the hat out of the guy's hands, knocking it high into the air. The jewel popped out, sparkling in the moonlight, as it spun above their heads. Everyone grabbed for it, but it was the captain, dazed and hot-sauce drunk, who nabbed it out of the tangle of desperate hands.

"Mine," said the captain, drool and spit spraying and dropping past his swollen lips. Then he tossed the green jewel into his mouth and swallowed.

"Ew," said Mike.

"Ew," echoed the nearest thug.

With the remaining goons unsure about what to do and the donkey's energy flagging, Mike realized it was time to get off this terrifying merry-go-round.

"Dani," called out Mike. "Let's go!"

"Okay!" Channeling a dancer's grace, Dani rolled back off the donkey and onto the cart.

"Jump!" screamed Mike. He, Dani, and Captain Kevin leapt off the rolling cart, landing hard and tumbling across the ground to the edge of the jungle.

Behind them, the cart, still full of dangerous scoundrels, swerved. The donkey turned and headed back toward town, and directly into Vincent and Rube's path. They looked up in shock as the donkey and its cart of jerks plowed directly into them, knocking the duo aside like bowling pins.

Meanwhile, Mike helped the captain and Dani get back to their feet and pushed them into the jungle. He hoped they could cover some ground before the muscle from the Taco Diablo recovered.

"Oh, my gosh," gasped Dani suddenly.

"What? What?" asked Mike, glancing around. "What is it?"

"I was kind of awesome back there."

Mike laughed. "Yes, you were."

He thought for a moment, trying to catch his breath and process what they'd just been through.

"I guess *we* were pretty awesome," Mike said, trying to hoist the captain up so his feet wouldn't drag in the dirt. "No thanks to this guy."

The corners of Mike's mouth drew up into a smile. But then he saw a flicker of firelight coming through the branches behind them. His heart sank.

Torch flame and menacing shadows. The goons they had evaded were now heading their way.

A cold fear replaced the momentary elation as four thugs broke through the trees and surrounded them. They'd never make it back to the *Roger Oberholtzer*. They'd never make it back to their parents. It was over.

Mike swallowed the dread in his throat as he watched the mercenaries steady themselves, a few holding out machetes the size of baseball bats.

"Oh, hi, guys," said the captain to the mob, tightening his grip on the kids' shoulders. "My mouth is a volcano!"

"Cough it up," said one of the hooligans, flashing black-and-gray teeth.

"That might take a minute," the captain replied, holding his stomach and belching. "How about a trade?"

He pushed Dani and Mike into the startled arms of their adversaries.

"Take the kids," said the captain, injecting his sales pitch with every bit of charisma he had left. "They're yours, free of charge. Just don't kill me."

The hair on the back of Mike's neck stood up and the knot in his stomach returned.

"Really, man?" asked the largest of the thugs. "We just want the jewel. But seriously? You would give up the kids?"

"I mean, I've already got two mouths to feed at home," said another goon, who scratched his chin as he contemplated the offer. "Just seems wrong."

"That's brutal, man," said another. "He like this all the time?"

"Apparently," Mike said flatly.

"But he does have his good qualities, too," Dani chimed in.

"So," said the captain. "Do we have a deal?"

Then, from out of nowhere, a voice shouted out in the darkness.

"No deal!"

Before anyone could react, there was another sound—of thick metal bouncing off bone, ringing like a wet church bell. The guy behind Mike collapsed.

Dani dropped down to her haunches as a frying pan flew out of the darkness and took out the baddie closest to her. He stumbled back into his comrade, both of them falling into the jungle brush, a jumble of limbs, pain, and bad smells.

"Hey," said the blind captain. "What's going on?"

But nobody answered him. He wasn't the only one who couldn't see this new adversary.

"Where are you?" belched the last standing mercenary. "Come out and fight like a man!"

"But I'm not a man," replied the voice. And the large frying pan rose up behind him and collided with the back of his oddly shaped head. *WHONGK!*

The noise made both Mike and Dani flinch.

The final mercenary closed his eyes, weapons slipping from limp hands. He fell into the brush like a lifeless marionette, revealing the woman standing behind him.

It was the waitress from Taco Diablo. Mike couldn't believe it. She'd saved them.

She was holding the frying pan in one hand and a white doggie bag in the other. She lifted the bag.

"You forgot your leftovers!"

CHAPTER 12
AND THEN THERE WERE FOUR

DANI STARED at the waitress. "You saved us."

"Hi," the waitress said awkwardly.

"I'm Dani," Dani said, suddenly a huge fan of this woman. "You were so great back there. You're supercool."

"*Um*, thanks," said the waitress. "We probably should get going."

The four of them made their way through the dark jungle and, at long last, back to the *Roger Oberholtzer*. Dani and the (supercool) waitress from the decrepit taco place helped get the captain aboard as Mike buzzed around the deck, his voice high and panicked. "Okay, time to get the show on the road and get this boat away from this place—not to mention all those people who wanted to kill you. And kill *us* because we were with you."

Dani looked over to see the captain at the wheel, fumbling with the ship's controls. His face looked like it had been kicked by an elephant—red and swollen and scrunched up. She watched as the captain rubbed his eyes, screamed, then rubbed his eyes again.

"Wash your hands!" hollered Mike, clearly exasperated.

"Maybe I should wash my hands," the captain said, and he stumbled toward the bathroom belowdecks.

The waitress/rescuer was untying the rope lines laced around the dock. She motioned to Dani. "Wanna give me a hand? The boys seem, uh, busy."

Dani kneeled down to help, turning to address the waitress with the frying pan skills. "Who are you?"

"My name is Aruna," she said.

"Are you an action hero?" Dani asked. "My favorite action hero is Bermuda Betty. Momo and I have read all the books. Well, she *was* my favorite till she disappeared into the Bermuda Triangle. You kind of look like her. Are you married?"

"*Um*," Aruna said. "Hi, Dani. Nice to meet you. I'm not sure I'm really the Bermuda Betty type."

"You definitely are," said Dani.

"Can I just ask . . ." Aruna started. "Who are you kids and what are you doing with that guy? Is he really your stupid uncle or something?"

"Who's a stupid uncle?" asked Captain Kevin, stumbling back onto the deck.

"He's not our uncle," said Dani, snickering. "But that would be cool if he was! He's Captain Kevin, and that's my brother, Momo."

"It's Mike, actually. And we've been kidnapped," said Mike as he scrambled to untie anything still securing the boat to the dock.

"No, no, no," Captain Kevin cried, still squinting through the pain the hot sauce had inflicted. "Never mind that. Who are *you*, and why did you save us?" He shook his finger at a lawn gnome strapped to a support strut.

"I'm over here," said Aruna.

The captain swiveled toward where he heard her voice.

"Who are you and why did you save us?" repeated Captain Kevin.

"Well, it's going to sound cheesy, but I've always wanted a life of adventure."

Dani gasped. "Me too! We could be sisters!"

"Can't we talk about all this once we're further down the river?" asked Mike.

Sometimes Dani wanted to punch Mike. This was one of those times.

So she did.

"Ow," said Mike.

"He's going to be impossible until we get moving," Dani sighed.

Working together, they quickly got the *Roger Oberholtzer* back on course and away from the village full of captain-haters. Once Dani could see her brother finally start to breathe again, she turned back to Aruna.

"So, what's your story, fellow adventure seeker?"

"I'll keep it brief," said Aruna. "Single child. Unfulfilled. Some college. Unfulfilled. Odd jobs. Unfulfilled. Bad vacation tour. Unfulfilled."

She sighed and leaned back against the railing.

"I didn't mean to land here, but that restaurant was where I ended up. Feels like I've been stuck in that place my entire life. Trapped with no future. Stuck and scared. Afraid to leave and try something else. Just another waitress, waiting for something."

She looked out across the vast river, the faraway moon reflected in her faraway gaze.

"I think I just needed to steer my own destiny."

Captain Kevin snorted, loudly and sarcastically.

"But then I saw you guys in trouble, and I knew I had to help. I wanted to take a risk and, I don't know, jump at the chance to do something amazing while it was in front of me. I didn't know what I was waiting for until today."

Aruna paused, and Dani saw Mike crinkle his brow.

"Great story. You done?" asked the captain. "Then we'll pull over and drop you off ashore."

"Look, now that I've helped you three, those guys are gonna be coming for me, too. I'm in as much danger as you are, so I have to keep moving," Aruna said firmly. "Where are you headed?"

"Treasure!" squealed Dani.

"Nowhere," corrected Captain Kevin. "We're going nowhere without the map. And besides, I've already got all the stowaways I need. Why should we adopt you?"

Aruna held up the to-go bag from the taco shop in a pose that Dani instantly recognized. Head tilted. Arms out. Hands up. To Dani it meant *Duhhhh*. She'd done the same thing to her brother often enough. And, like her brother, Captain Kevin didn't seem to be getting it.

He glared at the bag in Aruna's hand.

"I'm not really in the mood for tacos," said Captain Kevin, gesturing at his puffy face. "I've kind of had my fill."

Aruna dropped her arms and shook her head. She pulled a Taco Diablo menu out of the bag. Then it hit Dani; she realized what Aruna was showing them.

But the captain still didn't. "Look," he said, his words slurring around his swollen tongue. "If I'm not eating anything, why would I need a menu? I mean . . ."

Captain Kevin looked to Mike for support. Mike shrugged back.

Boys, thought Dani, exasperated.

Clearly at her breaking point, Aruna threw the bag of tacos at Captain Kevin's head.

"Hey!"

"THIS. IS. THE. MAP," said Aruna slowly, holding up the menu.

Dani ran up and took the bottom two corners of the menu, helping to spread it out.

"It's the menu on one side." Dani flipped it over, laying it out on the deck. "The map is on the other."

"Thank you," said Aruna. Dani and Aruna high-fived.

Captain Kevin and Mike scooted over and examined the menu under the light of a lantern. It was the same kid's menu activity place mat they'd seen before, but upon closer inspection, they saw the connect-the-dots section actually had coordinates and measurements on it. It was a real map; a *map* map.

"Exactly! A map hidden in plain sight," said Captain Kevin. "I knew it the whole time."

Dani and Aruna rolled their eyes in sync, and Captain Kevin winced as he screwed up his face in an odd expression.

"I can't really wink because I drank hot sauce with my eyes, but pretend I did."

"Well, I actually have some experience as a guide," said Aruna. "I can help get us there, if you let me come along."

"Okay!" exclaimed the captain. "We've got a menu map, the jewel to unlock the temple, and now a waitress-slash-guide!"

"Wahoo!" cried Dani.

"So, just like that she's part of the crew?" Mike asked before quickly turning to Aruna. "No offense. I mean, I'm glad you're here, and really glad you saved our lives. It's great to have you—"

"You're babbling," said Dani.

"I'll stop," said Mike.

"That's how adventures work!" the captain said, striking a heroic pose that he almost pulled off. "Unforeseen twists. Strange alliances. Unexpected snack breaks. It's all very mysterious."

Captain Kevin turned to look at Aruna. "But just so you know, I don't trust you as far as I can throw you."

"Oh, I don't trust you, either," she replied with a smile.

"Excellent!" he laughed. "Then off we go! Treasure, here we come! Waitress!"

"Aruna," said Aruna.

"Waitress Aruna," said Captain Kevin. "You've got the wheel because I am mostly blind. Dani, you're on map duty."

He tossed Dani a compass, which flew over her head and into the water.

PLOP.

"Cool!" said Dani.

"Wait," protested Mike. "You said after your little meeting you'd take us back to our parents."

"I said after the meeting *and* the treasure," Captain Kevin lied.

Mike made a noise that sounded like he was disgusted and exhausted at the same time. "UGHHFLAW!"

"Don't UGHHFLAW me," said Captain Kevin. "With those mercenaries after us, you and your sister are safer with me."

"Safer?" Mike balked. "But—"

"Look, kid. You can make this easier or be a big pain in my butt. Either way, I'm going to get that treasure, and I'm not taking you back until I get it," the captain said. "So, we'll all be a lot happier if you accept that, stop trying to mess everything up, and help. Okay?"

Mike kept his mouth shut.

Normally, this silent reaction would have comforted Dani. But she could tell by the look in her brother's eyes that his gears were moving. Mike was working something out in his head. Dani just wasn't sure what.

CHAPTER 13
GET RIGHT BACK TO WHERE WE STARTED

MIKE HAD A PLAN.

Captain Kevin was still in his quarters belowdecks, trying to rest his bloodshot eyes and wrecked body. Mike had heard the toilet flushing about seventeen times so far. The hot sauce had taken its toll.

It was the middle of the night. There would never be a better time.

Mike marched up to Aruna, who had been left at the helm, trying to figure out exactly what to say to her.

Maybe she is right, thought Mike. Maybe it was important to take a risk and steer your own destiny. Maybe now was Mike's chance to take matters into his own hands.

"I'm turning the boat around," he said firmly, or at least as firmly as he could manage. He was trying to sound confident, but he wasn't feeling that way. Maybe that's all being brave was—ignoring your stomach and faking the rest?

Aruna turned her huge brown eyes toward Mike; he felt as if two large spotlights had suddenly found him. The back of his neck was damp with sweat.

But then Aruna smiled.

It was a small smile, but enough of one that Mike thought Aruna looked a little surprised . . . and maybe even a little impressed.

"Really?" she asked. Her tone indicated to Mike that she wasn't asking for clarification. She had heard him; she just wanted to make sure he was sure.

"Why?" she continued.

"Because of what you said before, about taking a risk," Mike replied.

"That's not really what I meant," countered Aruna. But Mike had a head full of steam and a mouthful of words that needed to be said.

"We shouldn't be here," he said. "And the longer we are here, the more danger we'll be in. No one's gonna help Dani and I, so we need to help ourselves. If we turn around now, we can get back to our parents and then you and the captain can go off and do whatever it is he's trying to do. We're a burden anyway, I'm sure. It's the right thing."

"What about the treasure hunt and the jewel and—"

Mike huffed like a dog. "He ate the jewel."

Laughter exploded out of Aruna's face. She tried to catch it with her hand, but it was too late.

"He ate it?" she asked. "Really? That's where the jewel is?"

"Yeah, he swallowed it," said Mike. "But that's not really the point . . ."

"But even so, what twelve-year-old boy doesn't want to go on a treasure hunt?" she asked.

"It's not about me," said Mike. "It's Dani." Mike took a moment to find the words. "You said you don't have any brothers or sisters, right?"

"Right," Aruna said softly.

"Well, being a big brother means you protect your younger sibling," said Mike. "Which makes Dani my responsibility. And once, when I was eight and she was three, I was supposed to be watching her."

He paused, staring at the moon's reflection wobbling like Jell-O in the river water. It had been a long time since he'd shared this with anyone. He wasn't sure he wanted to, really, but the words came anyway.

"I messed up. Dani got hurt. She fell and we had to rush to the hospital, and I was really scared. She was okay, in the end, but . . . My parents trusted me, and I let them, and her, down. I promised I'd never let that happen again."

Aruna stared at him.

"That's messed up," she said finally.

"What?"

"Your parents were wrong," Aruna said. "That's too much responsibility for a kid your age. Eight-year-olds are supposed to be having fun, messing around, getting into trouble, not being in charge of another small human. A kid can barely take care of himself at that age. You really need to let yourself off the hook."

She looked over at Dani, who had climbed up onto the roof of the center hold and was trying to entice passing fireflies with a five-year-old Pop-Tart from the vending machine.

"Besides, that was years ago," Aruna said. "I think Dani can probably take better care of herself now."

"I don't know about that," said Mike. "But I have a responsibility to keep her safe, and that's what I'm going to do."

Aruna smiled again. "He swallowed the jewel? Really?"

Mike nodded.

"Well, sounds like you've thought a lot about this," said Aruna, holding Mike's gaze.

"I have," agreed Mike.

Aruna nodded, then stepped aside, offering him the wheel.

"Captain . . ."

Mike moved up to the wheel and Aruna showed him how to safely operate the boat in the dark. Gently and slowly, Mike eased the boat into a wide turn, Aruna helping him adjust their speed. The river was wide enough where they happened to be, so the turn wasn't that hard after all. Aruna stepped back, and suddenly Mike was driving the boat himself.

He felt older, like he was one step closer to being a teenager—or even an adult. It was easier than he thought, taking charge of his destiny.

Sailing up the Amazon under the light of the full moon, Mike was feeling pretty great about himself when he heard Dani's voice.

"What's going on?" she asked.

Dani stood on the deck with her hands on her hips and her chin cocked to one side like a loaded weapon. Her eyes bored into her brother's back with the fury of an eight-year-old girl who smelled something fishy . . . and it wasn't the Amazon.

Aruna, now resting on one of the deck chairs, pointed to Mike at the wheel.

"His idea," she said, not looking up from her comfortable repose.

"Momo?" asked Dani. "Why are we turned around? Are we going back?"

She saw his somber expression and instantly erupted. "No! No way!"

"Family meeting!" called Mike, trying to sell the idea that he was calling the shots now. "I got us into this, and I've got a plan to fix it."

"But the captain—" started Dani.

Mike cut her off. "The captain doesn't care about us, Dani. He cares about his jewel and his treasure. We're just in the way, and if we stay here, I'm worried that things are going to get worse and we might never get home."

Dani clenched her fists, tears collecting in her squinted eyes.

"You're not Mom and Dad, Momo!" she hollered, throwing a righteous finger in her brother's face.

"No," said Mike, picking his words carefully. "But they're not here. And we need to get back to them. That's enough adventure. For the both of us."

Dani stomped on Mike's foot.

"Ow!" hollered Mike.

Aruna stood up and looked ahead, worry crossing her face.

"Uh, kids?" said Aruna as she took back the wheel.

"I am not happy with you right now," Dani yelled at Mike,

before turning to Aruna. "Or you, either!" Dani looked down at the deck of the ship and stomped on it. "And I'm very disappointed in you, *Roger Oberholtzer*."

Suddenly, Mike heard a noise over the rush of the river and the hum of the boat's engines. It was something angry and loud.

"What is . . ." started Mike, but the noise became so loud it drowned him out.

Engines.

Actually, the growl of other boat engines. And they were getting louder.

"We've got company!" hollered Aruna over the din.

All three of them looked forward and saw the lights of a boat and several Jet Skis headed their way. Rube and the other miscreants from the taco place were slicing through the water with scowls on their faces—and drawing ever closer.

"Was this part of your plan?" asked Dani.

"Nope," said Mike, deflating like a balloon.

"Good one, bro," said Dani.

CHAPTER 14
BAD GUYS AND BOAT CHASES AND DANGER, OH MY!

"**W**E'RE ALL GONNA DIE!" screamed Mike. "Again!"

"Yeah!" hollered Dani over the rising roar of the bad guys' engines. "But this time it's your fault!"

"Aaarrgghh!" screamed Mike. "I know it's my fault! I can fix this!"

"How?"

Dani joined her brother at the wheel, trying to help him turn the boat away from the swarming attackers. There were four snarling vehicles in all—one skiff and three Jet Skis—and they were closing in quickly.

"Faster!" Aruna yelled as she ran to the railing, keeping her eyes on their new "friends." Mike nodded furiously and tried to push the engine harder.

"Faster, Mr. *Roger Oberholtzer*!" said Mike.

"I don't think he likes your tone," commented Dani.

"Please go faster, Mr. *Roger Oberholtzer*!" corrected Mike.

"Better," said Dani.

Mike thought he felt the boat speed up. But only a little.

Once they had pivoted and were headed back downriver, Dani rushed to Aruna's side at the rear of the boat to watch the mercenaries racing after them. The deep blue of the Amazon night was broken by the searchlights of the gas-powered skiff and the three headlamps on the Jet Skis. They were like big bright lightning bugs charging over the water.

Aruna pulled a rubber band out of her pocket and tied her long hair back into a high ponytail. Dani moved to do the same, and Aruna, without looking, handed her a rubber band the moment she needed it.

"Thanks," said Dani.

"A little faster please, *Roger*," Aruna said, patting the railing.

Mike shook his head, exasperated.

"It won't go any fast—"

Mike didn't even get to finish his sentence before the *Roger Oberholtzer* suddenly picked up speed. It was noticeable this time.

Mike's jaw dropped and he scowled at the boat.

"You like everyone better than me, don't you?" a stunned Mike asked the boat.

Then it sped up even more.

Mike glanced back. The mercenaries were within a few hundred feet now. The *Roger Oberholtzer* had bought them a little time and distance, but not much.

"You two better get below deck," Aruna said. "I'll handle this."

"But I wanna help," said Dani.

"No. Let me talk to them. I may know one or two of those hoodlums."

"How?" Mike asked.

"From the Taco Diablo. Now go."

"But someone has to steer the ship," Dani insisted.

Aruna sighed.

"Okay, fine. Mike, stay up by the wheel and keep us going straight. Dani, get below deck. Now."

They left Aruna at the back of the boat; Mike headed for the bridge, with Dani right behind him.

"Dani, she told you to go down where it's safe," admonished Mike.

"I know how to steer. And I think you better go wake the captain," she replied.

"What? What do we need him for?" Mike balked. "Seriously, how's he going to help? How does he *ever* help?"

"He helps!" Dani glowered at her brother.

"So why don't *you* go get him?" Mike protested.

"Hey!" Dani responded, taking a step closer to Mike. "You got us into this mess. Captain Kevin could get us out of it. Now go!"

"Ugh, fine." Mike turned on his heel, leaving Dani at the helm. He couldn't believe he had created a situation where they actually needed Captain Kevin.

He grumbled as he saw his frazzled reflection in the porthole-style window at the entrance to the lower deck. He grumbled as he stomped down the stairs. He grumbled as he pushed open the door to the captain's room to find the man still asleep in his spacious bunk.

The captain's private quarters, however, were a mess. Everything inside looked like it had been decorated by someone younger than Dani and had been broken and repaired at least twice. Christmas lights hung in the corner, and trash and old water bottles littered the floor. There were posters of old movies on the walls, not framed, but instead taped and stapled—their images of old adventurers faded from the windowlight and exposure to the elements.

Captain Kevin himself was sprawled out over his bed like a starfish, snoring—oblivious to the trouble brewing just outside. His cheeks were damp with sweat and his cap was still fastened to his head.

"Wake up, you idiot!" hollered Mike. "We're in trouble!"

Captain Kevin didn't budge. Or move. Or react in any way.

Mike moved closer to the captain, and his nose promptly wrinkled up at the smell he encountered. That couldn't be him, could it? Then he noticed that Captain Kevin was clutching a bucket of chum as if it were a teddy bear.

He was literally sleeping with the fishes.

Mike grabbed an oar leaning beside the bed, gripping it tightly with both hands. He felt so angry and frustrated that his teeth were practically vibrating. He was mad at Captain Kevin for his part in all of this, but truth be told, he was more upset with himself.

Mike hollered and beat the side of the bed with his oar. The mattress sloshed back and forth, rocking the captain like a dinghy on the high seas.

What? Mike thought. *A waterbed on a boat? Isn't that redundant?*

The captain snored on.

Outside, Mike could hear the buzzing of the bad guys' approaching vehicles. It sounded like they were now circling the boat with their Jet Skis, whooping and cheering.

Mike had been patient enough.

He took his oar and hit the captain's leg with it. *WHACK!*

"Wake up!"

Mike waited, but the captain still didn't stir.

So he hit the captain's chest with the oar, harder this time. *WHAP.*

Still nothing.

Mike popped the captain in the face with the oar. *WHAP!*

He immediately felt sorry. He'd gone too far. But the captain still hadn't woken up. Mike shrugged and looked around to see if anyone was watching. They weren't—so he hit the captain in the face again.

WHAP!

"Wake up!" hollered Mike.

He hit him again.

WHAP!

WHAP!

WHAP!

"What are you doing?" asked Dani.

Mike spun in place like a top, guilt and remorse blooming on his cheeks. He gripped the oar tightly to his chest and attempted an innocent smile, but his mouth wasn't cooperating.

"He's still asleep," said Mike.

"I can tell," said Dani, already hurrying back upstairs. "Come on. I think Aruna needs our help!"

Mike looked back at the snoring captain, and one more time popped him in the nose with the oar for good measure. *WHAP*. Then he ran back above deck.

Before his eyes could adjust to the dark tropical night, Mike sensed something large flying toward his head.

"Duck!"

"Duck?" asked Mike, though he dropped down just as Captain Kevin's cooler flew over his head. Aruna was swinging it on a rope like a ball and chain.

"I told you two to keep out of the way!" Aruna yelled.

She looked like an Amazon warrior, running across the deck of the ship, swinging the cooler above her head. "And I warned you worms to stay back!"

One of the Jet Ski goons pulled up to the right side of the boat. He reached out a muscled, tattooed arm and tried to grab the side railing. It was Rube, the scary singing guy from the taco shop.

"I did warn you," said Aruna, before loosening her grip on the line. The cooler careened through the air and into Rube, knocking him clean off his vehicle. He fell into the river, the abandoned Jet Ski turning and slowing, its engine sputtering to a stop with a satisfying choke and rumble.

Dani leapt high off the deck and yelped in triumph as Aruna pulled the cooler back aboard.

"Hey," Aruna yelled at the kids. "I told you. Get out of here!"

"We can help!" said Dani.

"Please don't," yelled Aruna.

"C'mon, Dani," said Mike as he pulled his sister toward the bow of the boat. "No one's steering the ship."

They hurried to the front of the boat, and Dani grabbed the wheel. Their view of the back of the boat, however, was blocked by the center hold, and they couldn't see how Aruna was doing. Mike leaned out over the railing to try to get a look.

"No, no, no, no, no!" he cried.

The gas-powered skiff was pulling alongside the *Roger Oberholtzer*. It was an oversized inflatable raft infested with bad guys, like a melted Popsicle swarming with ants. And Mike could see that the swarm was about to crash their picnic.

One of the thugs twirled a rope with a grappling hook on the end and let it fly. It snared the railing of the *Roger Oberholtzer*, and the man immediately started reeling the rope in, bringing the two boats closer.

"They're gonna board the boat!" Mike yelled.

Dani yanked the steering wheel hard to the right, then quickly back the other direction, rocking the boat and slamming it into the skiff. Most of the mercenaries on board toppled into the water just before their rubber vehicle capsized. Unfortunately, Dani's quick thinking also knocked Mike on his tail and sent Aruna flying overboard.

They heard her startled scream as she flew over the railing. Dani immediately let go of the wheel and ran to the back.

Mike joined his sister, gripping the rear railing tightly with both hands. He could see the anchor chain—one end still attached to the boat, the other end dragging in the river.

But there was no Aruna. He watched the two remaining Jet Ski buddies drop to the rear, where the anchor line hit the water. They were looking for signs of the waitress, too.

Mike and Dani frantically scanned the water for her in the darkness. It was as if the river had swallowed her whole. Mike's worried thoughts darted around in his head: Had she drowned? What would they do if she was really gone? What if those men actually got on board? What then? What would happen to them?

Instinctively, Mike grabbed Dani's little hand and squeezed.

As one of the men leaned down toward the anchor in the water, a fist burst up out of the river and caught the goon on the chin. It knocked him backward, as if he were a stuffed doll.

Suddenly, Aruna's head came up for air—and Mike and Dani breathed with her.

"Aruna!" they both cheered. Mike could actually feel the color coming back to his bleached-out cheeks as relief flooded his body.

"Stop helping and get below!" shouted Aruna. "Am I not speaking English?"

They stared, almost as if they were watching a movie with a real-life action hero. Aruna held fast to the anchor chain with one hand, then pulled behind the *Roger Oberholtzer*. With her other hand, she grabbed hold of the Jet Ski closest to the boat, pushed the unconscious rider into the river, and pulled herself up and onto it.

There was one Jet Ski jerk who tried to swipe at her with

his free hand. But he missed and swerved, giving Aruna time to swivel into position on her newly commandeered vehicle. She wrapped the anchor chain to the Jet Ski's steering column as she settled into position, towed behind the larger ship. It was like watching Olympic gymnastics on television; Aruna's body moved effortlessly and did only what it needed to do, with no extra movement, graceful and lyrical in its execution. It was really, really cool.

Suddenly, the *Roger Oberholtzer* grunted and Mike heard the bite of breaking wood and metal. Both kids ran forward to the bow of the boat and saw that the ship had drifted, driverless, into rough currents scraping over jagged rocks.

Aruna yelled something.

But Mike couldn't quite make it out. As he turned to face her, something huge and wet wrapped around his neck and pulled him off his feet.

FROM THE JOURNAL OF CAPTAIN
KEVIN ADVENTURESON

ZZZZZZZZZZZ. ZZZZZ. ZZZZZZZZZZ.

CHAPTER 15
WE'RE ALL GONNA DIE, PART 2

AS HE FLEW BACKWARD, Mike finally realized that Aruna had yelled, "Behind you!"

But now it was too late.

Mike grabbed at the fleshy thing around his neck. It was an arm. A tattooed arm.

Rube.

The gangster Aruna had taken out with the cooler had clearly survived and then stealthily made his way aboard the *Roger Oberholtzer*.

Rube was just as intimidating as he had been before, only now he was wet. And angry, like a house cat on bath day. Strangely, Mike's brain registered that Rube's breath still smelled of peppermint as he slammed Mike up against the vending machine. Behind him the junk food jostled in its metal lanes and the resident snake, still in the machine, dropped its coiled body from B3 to D6.

Rube hummed a pleasant tune, then applied more pressure to Mike's chest with his giant ham-shaped forearm.

"That's excessive," squeaked Mike. "I already can't breathe."

"But you can talk," said Rube. "So, talk. Where is it?"

"Where is what?" asked Mike, adding quickly, "Please don't kill me."

"Please don't *make* me," replied Rube, a song in his voice. He pushed harder on Mike's chest. "Now. The jewel."

Mike was panicking. He didn't know what to do. Black clouds were collecting at the corners of his vision. He was blacking out.

Mike thought quickly. He should just tell Rube where the jewel was. Mike was not currently Captain Kevin's biggest fan anyway. But instinct, and all the pulp-adventure novels he had read, told him that revealing the location of the jewel to this brute wouldn't really help anything. Peppermint breath or not, Rube was bad news. But what could Mike do?

Then he noticed the snake again, wrapping itself around the potato chips hanging loosely from the end of D6.

"Spill," snapped Rube.

Suddenly, Dani was on the man's back, hammering at the back of his head with an oar. *WHAP, WHAP, WHAP!*

"Ow," growled Rube. Even this sounded like a threat.

"Dani, no!" cried Mike.

But there was nothing he could do as Rube, with one arm still pinning Mike to the vending machine, shrugged Dani off his back. He knocked her off her feet with one small flex of his substantial back and shoulders.

"You're next, hot-sauce girl." Rube treated Dani to his winning smile.

Mike knew he had to act now. With as little movement as

possible, Mike reached for the loose change in his pocket and fed it into the vending machine, even while pinned by the tattooed ruffian. He snuck a peek at the keypad and hit D6. He heard his selection drop down into the retrieval bin.

Dani leapt to her feet and growled at Rube, but he grabbed her around the neck with his meaty paw.

Rube lifted her up off the deck.

Mike saw Dani's eyes water. She was choking, her face red like a ripe apple. Mike winced as the man turned back and reapplied pressure to Mike's chest with his other chunky arm.

"And you," said Rube. "Enough squirming. Where's the jewel?"

"I know where it is," Mike began.

"Momo, no," said Dani in a quiet, choked voice. She looked so small in Rube's deadly grip, tears carving dirt-streaked lines on her face. It broke something inside Mike to see his sister in pain, and a fire burned behind his eyes. He pulled his mouth into a hard line.

"It's in here," said Mike, reaching behind him toward the vending machine.

Rube let Mike down, releasing the pressure from his huge arm. "Give."

Without thinking, Mike plunged his hand down into the retrieval bin, grabbed the snake, and threw it at Rube.

The large man's reaction was more than Mike could have hoped for. He screamed like one of those goats on the Internet, jarringly and outrageously loud, then dropped Dani back to the deck, where she got the chance to catch her breath.

Rube threw his arms up to protect his face, instantly

providing plenty of juicy places for the snake to bite. And bite it did. Rube backpedaled in a blind panic, the snake hanging on to his bicep by its clenched teeth. Moving quickly, Dani scrambled behind Rube on her hands and knees.

"Mike!" she called.

Mike acted on instinct, shoving Rube as hard as he could. Rube toppled backward, over Dani and then over the railing, taking his new snake pal with him.

Mike and Dani stared at each other with wide eyes as the screaming man was pulled into the river and vanished. Dani hugged her brother tightly.

Mike barely hugged back, overwhelmed.

"Did I just do that? Did I just grab a *snake*?" he muttered in a daze. "What was I thinking?"

"You guys okay?!" It was Aruna.

They ran to the back of the boat, where she was trailing behind them on the stolen Jet Ski. She held the anchor line still tethered to the boat, using it to keep pace like a water-skier. Mike looked out across the water and saw that she was the last one standing.

The goons were gone.

Putting their feet up against the railing for leverage, the kids pulled Aruna closer to the *Roger Oberholtzer*. She kicked free of her improvised water ski, lifted herself over the railing, and fell onto the deck and onto the kids.

They all took a moment to breathe, half from the effort and half from relief. Finally, Mike sat up, using one of the oars as a brace. He'd never felt so tired in his life.

They didn't notice that Captain Kevin had returned from belowdecks.

"You guys," he said, yawning and stretching. "I thought I asked you to keep it down. I was trying to catch forty winks."

"We'll try and be more careful next time," Mike replied, his words dripping with sarcasm.

"See that you do," said the captain, adjusting his jaw with his hand. "Why does my mouth taste like wood?"

Mike averted his eyes and carefully moved his oar out of sight.

CHAPTER 16
DAWN BREAKS LIKE AN IDIOT

THE BRAZILIAN SUN crept up over the horizon like a jaguar.

As the caws and cries of the waking jungle creatures cut through the thick, humid air, Dani kept her eyes focused on her prey.

"Aaaaiiee!" screamed Aruna.

She lunged forward, her hand like a cobra flying at Dani's neck.

Dani squealed, launching her left arm up and out, blocking the blow.

Amid the long morning shadows that stretched across the back of the boat, Dani and Aruna circled each other, their hands raised for attack, eyes squinting against the rising dawn.

When Dani had first asked Aruna to teach her some "cool moves," the woman had shrugged Dani off, then politely declined, and finally told her *no* in multiple languages. But Aruna had no idea how persistent the young girl could be once she put her mind to something.

Once, when Dani was four, her parents had told her she couldn't leave the table until she ate her vegetables. With the determination of a freckle-faced bulldog, Dani had slowly dragged the entire dining room table with her, inch by inch, into the family room so she could watch TV. She was not the type to give up.

Dani wanted to move like Aruna, fight like Aruna, do everything like Aruna—and her good-natured badgering had eventually worn the woman down. Now it looked like Aruna was actually enjoying the training session as much as Dani was.

"That's it. You trust your gut. That's good," Aruna said. "Now keep moving. Eyes on me at all times. You never know when I might—*strike!*"

Aruna's foot flew forward, her leg like a missile. Dani instantly dropped to the deck, the way Aruna had shown her, and simultaneously swung her leg around, knocking Aruna's feet out from under her. Aruna crashed to the deck beside her.

"It worked!" Dani giggled.

"You're doing great," Aruna smiled as she sat up. "Like a real-life Bermuda Betty."

Dani felt the heat rush into her face and knew that she was blushing. Over her short eight years of life, she'd been called "cute" and "smart" and even "daring," but Aruna had just given her the greatest compliment she'd ever gotten—ever.

As Dani struggled to find the words to reply, she suddenly felt her nose crinkle up at the harsh smell of smoke.

"What is that?" she asked.

Aruna sprang to her feet, pulling Dani up beside her.

"Something's burning," Aruna said.

They rushed toward the front of the boat. Captain Kevin stood at the bow, frantically pouring coolers full of water onto a sputtering fire. Smoke and steam billowed from the burnt carcass of a giant anaconda, nearly twenty feet long, the jungle wind carrying the odor of charred beast off the ship and down the winding river.

"What's going on?" Aruna asked.

"Yeah, what's going on?" Dani echoed. She could taste the snaky smoke in the back of her throat.

"Breakfast is served!" the captain called. "I have bravely captured and subdued a mighty creature of the Amazon for your dining pleasure. From now on, call me Captain Cook!"

Dani was confused. It looked like Captain Kevin had burnt their meal beyond recognition and had nearly set the whole boat on fire. But he was way too experienced to do something like that, right? Even now, he was stomping out embers of burning reptile on the deck.

"You want us to eat a snake?" said Dani as she stared at the long, twisted body over the fire. Her face screwed up like she'd just sucked on a lemon.

"Well, it wouldn't hesitate to eat you," the captain said. "Besides, it's delicious. And for dessert, we can bake a fresh apple *pie*-thon. Or a *bananaconda* cream pie. Or a pineapple upside-down *snake*."

Dani's brother poked his head up from belowdecks, rubbing the sleep out of his eyes with one hand while dragging his backpack of books with the other.

"Are we on fire?" Mike asked.

"Our appetites are!" Captain Kevin replied. "Now, who wants a snake steak, very, very, very, very, very, very, very very well-done?"

"Oh, no," Mike groaned, his eyes now wide.

"So it's a little burnt around the edges," the captain said. "It's what chefs on the Food Network call 'blackened.'" To Dani, the snake looked like the burned burgers her father served from time to time—if those burgers had been ten feet long and scaly.

"Not that," Mike said, his voice trembling as he pointed over the bow. "That!"

They looked out across the water, where Mike had spotted the first of several lizard-like behemoths heading for their boat. Like eerie black torpedoes, their snouts and slitted yellow eyes cresting the surface of the water, the deadly creatures moved in on the *Roger Oberholtzer* from every side.

"Alligators?" Dani asked, unconsciously taking a step back.

"Ha!" the captain laughed. "There are no alligators in the Amazon."

"Oh, good." Dani felt her muscles relax.

"That's a black caiman," Captain Kevin informed her. "Makes an alligator look like a prancing French poodle. Largest predator in the Amazon. Must've smelled the burning meat."

"Gee, ya think?" Mike shot back. "Those things are huge! Like *Journey to the Center of the Earth* dinosaur huge. And I'm talking about the Jules Verne book, not the movie. The book goes into much more detail about the actual scale of—"

"Momo." Dani brought Mike back to the problem at hand.

"Right, right. We have to do something. There's four, five of 'em heading our way," Mike counted. "And another bunch over there!"

"Oh, and those are just the ones you can see!" the captain said mischievously. The dull brown water of the river hid its secrets well, and Dani realized he was right; she had no way of knowing what else lurked below the surface.

"Seventy-six teeth," Mike said to himself.

"What?" Dani asked.

"Each one of those ferocious beasts has seventy-six sharp, lethal teeth crammed into its powerful, skull-crushing jaws."

"Don't tell me. You read all about it," she sighed.

"And with nine, ten . . . eleven of them," Mike counted, "that makes eight hundred thirty-six ways they could puncture us."

"Fear not," Captain Kevin said, leaning back against the railing. "I got this."

Dani couldn't believe how brave he was.

"In all my years as an adventurer, I've never been killed by one of these guys," he bragged. "Every time, they *caiman* went. They came and went? See what I did there? You see, I—"

Captain Kevin was cut off mid-sentence as eleven hundred pounds of reptilian muscle launched out of the water, tongue out and limbs sprawled wide. The captain jerked back just as the ferocious jaws of the beast snapped shut right where his noggin had been. Flecks of river water and saliva flew from the creature's mouth, spattering across the face that the captain had nearly lost.

"Keep away from the sides!" the captain yelled as he fell back onto his butt and crab-walked away from the edge as fast as he possibly could.

The *Roger Oberholtzer* was under attack.

CHAPTER 17
THEY CAIMAN THROUGH THE BATHROOM WINDOW

DANI SCREAMED.

All around the boat, the huge creatures burst from the water, jaws snapping like deadly castanets, the deadly rhythm of their clapping mouths synchronized to the pounding beat of Dani's heart. The railing shattered under the staggering weight of one of the reptiles as it heaved its bulky body aboard the *Roger Oberholtzer*.

"Retreat!" the captain screamed, running past the kids to dive belowdecks.

To some it might have looked like Captain Kevin was running away like a terrified titmouse, but Dani could tell he was valiantly leading them to safety. Or at least she hoped so.

She felt Mike push her through the doorway, his bag of books smacking her in the back as they ran. Aruna was right on his heels and slammed the door behind them.

"This won't hold long," she warned from the stairs, peering through the small window to the deck. "Not if they come after us."

"They're just hungry," Dani suggested, crowding in beside Aruna on the steps to see.

"They want the snake?" Mike said. "Let 'em have the stupid snake."

Peering up through the porthole window in the door, Dani could see more and more of the caimans clambering onto the deck and making their way toward the smoldering anaconda carcass.

Dani couldn't help shivering as the largest of the monsters hinged open its jaws and, moving faster than she could have imagined, sank its razor-sharp teeth into the snake flesh. This seemed to be the cue for the rest of the pack. They lunged at the charred body, attacking in a feeding frenzy.

"Caimans, party of five. Your table is ready," said the captain, as he squeezed in between the ladies to watch. "They certainly appreciate fine dining more than *some* people."

But the captain had spoken too soon.

The hungry reptiles suddenly stopped their feast, letting the snake's corpse fall half eaten from their mouths.

The group's leader, the gargantuan gator that had led the feast, spat out a bulky, half-chewed piece, coughing and hacking to rid its mouth of the remnants.

"Oh, come on!" the captain protested. "What's wrong with my cooking?"

"You burnt it," hissed Aruna, trying not to raise her voice.

"I told you: 'blackened'! It's a delicacy!"

The largest caiman turned toward the sound of the captain's barking. Its eyes narrowed as it saw the humans staring back through the tiny window in the door.

Dani met the prehistoric creature's gaze. It issued a thick gargling hiss and led its fellow man-eaters toward their new potential four-course meal.

"Oh, crap on a stick," the captain whined, running down the stairs to his cabin.

"Go!" Aruna barked, ushering the kids in the same direction.

"No, no, no," Captain Kevin protested. "No one is allowed in the captain's quarters except for the captain. Otherwise, they would call it the 'captain and friends' quarters, or the 'everybody come on in' quarters, or—"

They piled inside anyway. Dani slammed the door shut as Mike and Aruna grabbed a dresser from across the room.

"Barricade it," Mike yelled. "Grab everything you can."

Dani seized the end table beside the captain's bed. She was about to hurl it toward the door when she stopped, frozen in place. Propped on the table was a framed black-and-white picture of a grinning family. Clearly, it was the picture that had come with the frame, but Captain Kevin's face had been taped onto one of the figures.

"Ohhhhh," Dani said, her voice caught in her throat. "That's so sad."

"You didn't see that!" The captain snatched up the picture and stuffed it under his pillow.

Captain Kevin's bed and end table joined the dresser as the group barricaded themselves inside. Dani grabbed a crate filled with the captain's unwashed unmentionables that smelled so bad she had to breathe through her mouth as she pushed it into place.

A crash reverberated throughout the boat. The largest caiman broke through the first doorway and threw its bloated body down the steps to the lower deck, searching for its prey.

"Whoa!" Dani marveled, a hint of excitement in her voice. "Did you feel the floor shake?"

"You're not scared?" Aruna asked as she added her body weight to the pile of furniture blocking the entrance.

"She thinks this is an adventure," Mike explained. "She doesn't know enough to be scared."

"I know things," Dani spat back. "You don't know enough to be brave."

It was a mean thing to say, she knew. She didn't really believe it, but she hated when he talked to her like she was a dumb little kid. She was about to apologize when—

WHAM!

Something threw itself against the cabin door and the furniture jumped forward.

"Oh, crap," Dani said.

"Don't say 'crap,'" Mike said.

"Don't tell me what to do." Dani stuck out her tongue and blew a raspberry.

WHAM! The door took another hit.

"Is there any other way out of here?" Aruna asked, her eyes searching the room.

"The portholes?" Dani suggested.

WHAM! The door buckled under another assault and the hinges ripped free, spraying the room with splinters.

"Abandon ship!" Captain Kevin cried, rushing to throw open the nearest window. An angry caiman rammed its huge head through the porthole, cracking through the brittle wood, hungry jaws snapping wildly.

"What is this boat made of?" Mike cried. "Toothpicks?"

WHAM! The third and final attack on the cabin door ripped it free, toppling the hastily assembled wall of furniture. Standing in the doorway was the pack leader, its body backlit by the morning sun.

Dani squealed and scrambled with the others away from the predators, into the corner of the room.

There was no way out.

Another of the beasts entered through the doorway, joining its two comrades as they moved in on the surrounded humans.

"I got this!" said the captain as he quickly riffled through his pockets, searching desperately for something.

"I knew Captain Kevin would save us!" Dani cried.

His hand emerged from his pocket and rose up over his head, holding what looked like an explosive of some sort.

"Uh, can we stop and think about this first?" Mike said.

"No," the captain replied. "Sorry about this, *Roger.*"

Captain Kevin pulled a pin on the explosive, dropped it on the floor, and quickly threw a bucket over it.

"What are you—"

Dani's question was interrupted by a blinding, ear-shattering explosion. The reptiles recoiled. The bucket launched into the air like a rocket, and the bottom of the boat blew apart, leaving a three-foot hole torn from its hull. The river water burst through like a geyser.

"Are you insane?" hollered Aruna. "What are you doing?"

"I'm leaving," said the captain, bowing. "Thank you and good night!"

And with that, Captain Kevin dove out through the bottom of the sinking boat and into the bubbling water, leaving them alone with the monster reptiles.

"He left us," Dani whimpered in disbelief. "He left us!"

"Really?" Mike shook his head. "*That's* the part that's bothering you?"

FROM THE JOURNAL OF CAPTAIN
KEVIN ADVENTURESON

In my amazing travels across the globe, people ask me one question above all others: "Captain Kevin, where's the poop deck?"

But the *second* most asked question is equally profound: "What is the most important trait of a true Shipwrecker?"

Many people assume that it's my swagger, my dashing good looks, or my way with the ladies. But no.

It's courage.

Facing your fears. Looking death in the eyes and laughing. The bravery to stand fast, never to turn tail, never to run away, never to abandon ship. That is the most important trait of a Shipwrecker.

Never ever abandon ship.

Courage in the face of impossible odds can look a lot like stupidity. But it's not. At least, not usually.

My middle name, for a number of reasons that I won't get into, is Pamela. But I often tell people that my middle name is Courage.

Because it should be.

I also tell people my middle name is Poop Deck, but that's just because it's funny.

Poop Deck. Ha!

CHAPTER 18
THINGS ARE GOING SWIMMINGLY

MIKE BROKE THE SURFACE of the water, gasping for breath and shocked to still be alive.

"Dani!" The second his lungs were filled with air, his thoughts returned to his sister. Where was she? Had she made it?

Back on the boat, Aruna had held off the caimans long enough for the kids to dive into the hole Captain Kevin had blown open. But with all the dangers hiding in the Amazon River, Mike was worried they were jumping out of the frying pan and into the fire—a wet, piranha-filled fire.

"Dani!" he called again.

His heart seized up. He'd been so focused on getting off the boat and reaching the surface . . .

I got distracted, he thought. *Again. She was my responsibility and I lost her. What if—*

"Momo!" a familiar voice called back.

It was Dani. She was alive. Her head bobbed in the water like a cork with a bad case of bed head.

"Are you okay?" Mike yelled.

"Of course," she called back. "What? You didn't think I could do this?"

"No! Nobody can do this. It's insane!"

"I'm fine," she called, swimming toward him. "As long as there aren't any more caimans."

"Don't worry," came Captain Kevin's voice from the shore. He was already out of the river, feet planted firmly on dry ground. "They're all on the boat."

Before Mike could start yelling at the captain for abandoning them, he heard the distinct splashes of the reptiles abandoning the *Roger Oberholtzer*.

"Uh, never mind," Captain Kevin muttered.

"Swim, Dani!" Mike yelled. "Swim for it!"

Mike kicked as hard as he could. Soon his fingers touched the leaves of a bromeliad plant on the shore. His feet found the bed of the river and he clambered for dry land, pulling his sopping bag of books up with him. (He had thought for a second about leaving them behind, but when it came down to it, he just couldn't. They were all that he had left to keep him sane.)

Above Mike on the shore, Captain Kevin lifted his hand toward the boy.

Mike reached for it, but the captain's "helping hand" wasn't actually there for him; he was waving goodbye to the *Roger Oberholtzer*.

"So long, old chum," Captain Kevin said soberly as he watched his damaged boat drifting aimlessly downstream.

"If you love something, let it go. If it comes back to you . . . well, that seems unlikely now, doesn't it?"

Grumbling under his breath, Mike managed to pull himself up onto the riverbank and then turned to help Dani.

"Almost there!" Dani grinned as she neared the shore, unaware of the bright yellow eyes closing in behind her.

The caiman leapt from the water.

Mike grabbed Dani's hand and yanked her forward with all his might, but the caiman was fast. Mike's efforts seemed too little, too late.

His whole body went rigid with fear.

But suddenly, a heavy brown boot flew past Dani's head and into the predator's snout, slamming its mouth closed and knocking it off its deadly course.

Aruna. Somehow, she'd escaped the other caimans, gotten to shore, and was there at the exact instant when the kids needed her most.

That is one incredible waitress, thought Mike.

"Keep moving," she said, pulling Dani up to shore. "They aren't restricted to the water."

The foursome moved quickly away from the water's edge.

"Wow, I thought you were a goner," Captain Kevin admitted to Aruna as they hiked up the bank. "You must've been a cat in another life. You know, because of your nine lives. And all the hair balls."

Dani laughed.

"No," Mike interrupted, dripping with equal parts water and aggravation. "No way. You do not get to weasel out of this with a joke."

"How about two jokes? A priest, a rabbi, and a free-range chicken walk into a bar . . ."

"No! You almost got us killed. Again! And then abandoned us to die!" snarled Mike. "That was a new low, even for you!"

"I'm not going to dignify that with a response," Captain Kevin said. "I know you're just lashing out because of the pain you feel now that the *Roger Oberholtzer* is gone."

Mike's mouth hung open. The guy was like a serving of monkey brains without the brains.

"My ship. My home. My friend. Gone." The captain was despondent.

"You destroyed your own boat, you idiot," Aruna yelled. "What kind of moron does that?"

Mike felt something bubbling up inside him against his will. It was pushing the anger he had been holding aside like unwanted brussels sprouts. It was laughter.

"You sank your own boat," Mike laughed. He couldn't explain why, but the image of this dolt fearfully blowing up his prized possession struck him as the most idiotic, hilarious thing he'd ever seen. He fell to the ground, clutching his sides, his backpack landing beside him. "You sank. Your own. Boat!"

"Uh, not very sensitive, Momo," Dani whispered, her eyes darting from her brother to Captain Kevin and back again.

"It's over!" Mike chortled, making the smallest possible effort to regain control of himself. "There's no boat. He has to take us back now." Mike wasn't sure who he was trying to convince—Dani and the captain, or himself.

"What?" Captain Kevin raised his eyebrows in surprise.

"The boat's gone," argued Mike. "No more river

expeditions. No more crazy treasure hunts. We get to go back now. It's over!"

"Over?" Now the captain laughed. "What are you talking about? We're just getting started! Didn't you listen to anything I said during the tour? The shipwreck is inevitable. It's essential! It's the key, the catalyst, the turning point that propels us through the rest of the adventure!"

"Yeah," Dani piped up. "After the wrecked ship is when the real adventure starts!"

"Sorry, Momo." Captain Kevin smiled. "This is when it gets good."

As if to demonstrate, the captain patted his belly and moved a few feet down toward the river, then back up a few feet toward the jungle. He continued to rub his stomach, lurching back and forth like a rabid ocelot. He moved back toward the jungle and belched loudly.

"The jewel says this way!" shouted the captain as he moved toward the tree line. "Come on!"

"Aaaaaaaaaaaaaaaaaaaaaaaaaaaaaaaaaaaaaaaaaaugh!" Mike was screaming now.

His sister took a step toward him, but the look in his eye told her now was not the time.

"You! You!" Mike scrambled up the shoreline, stopping inches from Captain Kevin. His eyes narrowed, fists curled into throbbing weapons of mass destruction. "You're a liar. And an idiot. You think you're clever, but you're easily the stupidest person I've ever met! You put my sister's life in danger! You put all our lives in danger!"

"Oh, yeah?" the captain spat. "Well, who was the dummy

who turned the ship around and got us attacked? You! Ha! And who did I have to save when he was nearly eaten by a hippo? You!"

"Because you pushed me into the river!" Mike's eyes were bulging, his teeth bared.

"Because you deserved it!" Captain Kevin snarled, flecks of spittle flying from his lips.

They were face-to-face now, millimeters away from bumping noses.

Mike felt a hand on his arm. He spun around with a growl, ready to lash out.

It was Dani.

"Family meeting," she said softly.

Mike stared at her, trembling with fury. But he let his sister lead him away from the others, stomping behind her.

"Look, Momo, I know you're upset. I mean, it's super-obvious you're upset," said Dani, her voice even and quite mature for her age. "I thought, jeez, that little vein in your head is gonna burst, which would have been really gross, right?"

Her brother glared at her.

"And it's okay, really, but yelling and screaming isn't going to help us. And when you think about it, neither is trying to stop Captain Kevin."

Mike opened his mouth to protest, to yell, to call Captain Kevin a few dozen names—including ones his parents had forbidden him to use, but Dani put her finger to his lips.

"Just listen. We've tried it your way, more than once, and it's been . . . not good. It slowed us down; it put us in danger. It's not working. So, now we're doing it my way."

Mike's head shot back. *We're doing what now?*

"We're going with Captain Kevin," she continued. "We're going to find this treasure. And then we'll get back to Mom and Dad."

Again, Mike opened his mouth, a full seven and a half different reasons running through his mind as to why this was the absolute worst idea in the history of bad ideas. But Dani wasn't done.

"Look, the way I see it, the worst thing that can happen is we have a real-life adventure. Together!"

"No, the worst thing is we could die," Mike said.

Mike recoiled from the spray as Dani blew a raspberry at him.

"Momo! Snap out of it. This is an adventure! You always say there are no more adventures in the world, but, hey, surprise, look around—you're in one! Right here, right now, you are on an adventure!"

For the third time in as many minutes, Mike started to protest, but then stopped.

He couldn't help wondering: was she right?

He'd always believed that since there were no adventures left, there was no point in taking chances. Right? Why take a risk if there was no reward? And that belief had kept him out of a lot of sticky situations over the years.

But if adventures really *did* exist, what excuse did he have for playing it safe?

"She's right, m'boy," Captain Kevin said, intruding on their chat. "Some say 'nothing ventured, nothing gained.' But I say, nothing adventured, nothing *adgained.*"

CHAPTER 19
A GRAVE ENCOUNTER

THE JUNGLE SWALLOWED THEM SLOWLY.
Like an anaconda, it was hot, it was green, and it was twisting. And the long walk was the perfect opportunity for girl talk.

"So." Dani smiled mischievously as they waded through the dense foliage. "How do you feel about Captain Kevin?"

"What?" Aruna said. "What do you mean?"

"You know, do you like him?" asked Dani. "Or maybe *like* like him?"

If Aruna had been drinking something, she would have done a spit take right then and there.

"You do like him," Dani said, smiling. "Oh, I'm so *shipping* you two. No, even better, I'm gonna *shipwreck* you two so you never drift apart!"

Aruna shivered at the thought, a look of disgust on her face.

"That's, um, cute, Dani, but you are *so* far off base. Way, way, way off base. Way, way, way, way, way, way, way."

Dani laughed.

The more time they spent together, the more Dani liked

Aruna. Not only had she taught Dani some fighting moves, and saved her life—which was *huge*—but she also didn't treat Dani like a little kid. She didn't talk down to her the way most adults did. Aruna treated her more like, well, more like a sister.

"But since we're asking questions, who is he to you?" asked Aruna. "To you and your brother?"

Dani shrugged as she scuttled over a fallen log.

"Oh, we're just friends, so don't worry, he's all yours."

"No," Aruna said. "Ew. I mean, you really just met him? You're not involved in his treasure hunt? Not part of his scheme, at all?"

Dani shook her head.

"And the jewel he keeps talking about," Aruna pressed. "He actually swallowed it? You mean, like, it's in his stomach?"

"Yup, I saw him do it." Dani nodded. She thought it was an odd question, but she let it go. There were a lot of other things in the jungle to pay attention to instead. Lots of *weird* things, including a massive tree that appeared to be upside down.

"Are those roots?" Dani asked as she caught up to her brother.

"I guess so." Mike shrugged, not really looking. "Why?"

"Because shouldn't they be on the ground?"

Dani was pointing straight up.

"That's crazy," Aruna said, staring up in wonder.

"I've—I've never read about anything like this," Mike stammered.

The tree was easily one hundred feet tall, its trunk as thick as a building. But where its branches should have been reaching for the sky, there were twisted roots, dark with jungle soil.

"I believe that's the pineapple upside-down tree," the captain explained. "Leaves and branches at the bottom and everything else pointing upward. Scientists studied it for years from ground level and never could get to the *root* of the problem. But they may have been *barking* up the wrong tree."

"Amazing how long he can talk with no knowledge whatsoever," Aruna whispered.

"It's incredible," Mike said, but he wasn't talking about the captain. His head was in the trees.

"I've never seen anything so weird." Dani grinned.

"Uh, then you might want to look in the mirror," Mike said.

"Ha ha, very funny."

"No, I'm serious. Your hair. It's standing straight up!"

Dani's dark curly hair was really levitating, lifting up from the sides of her head and pointing in every direction. She couldn't see herself, but she could feel the hairs rising on the back of her neck.

"What's happening? Momo, what is this?"

"I don't know. Maybe—maybe it's just static electricity. You know. Like when you rub your head with a balloon or touch one of those static-electricity generators they have on TV."

"Well, whatever it is, it's happening to you, too!" Dani said.

She watched Mike's disheveled mop lift off his head like the hair of a mad scientist in a monster movie.

"Whoa!" Mike was patting his giant head of hair with a silly grin on his face.

"What do you think it is, Captain Kevin?" Dani asked.

"No idea," he said, waving his hand over their heads as if to check for invisible wires. "That is some *weiiiird* hocus-pocus."

The captain gestured to the area around them as he led them on.

"But this is a weird hocus-pocus type of place. This area in particular is legendary for strange and unusual occurrences. In fact, it's often referred to as 'Freaky-Deaky Town' or 'Messed-up-potamia.'"

Dani laughed at that, though she wasn't sure she really understood the joke. To her surprise, Aruna laughed, too, but she covered her mouth with her hand to keep the captain from seeing.

"Good news, though," said the captain, patting the jewel in his tummy. "It means we're close!"

He pushed back a large palm frond and nearly walked straight into a towering figure. He froze, face-to-face with a hideous woman, her skin gnarled like wood, her features worn and broken. One eye stared down at him in accusation. Where the other eye should have been, there was a dark, empty socket that disgorged a scurrying centipede.

The captain screamed.

He stumbled backward into Aruna and the kids.

Intrigued, Dani pushed him out of the way to get a closer look.

"It's a ship!" she cried. "A big old pirate ship!"

The thing that had freaked the captain out was actually the masthead on the front of a ship—a large wooden woman whose features had been worn away by time and the sea. The overgrown foliage had hidden the rest of the vessel from view, and even now as Captain Kevin approached her for a second time, he seemed scared. He knocked on her stomach to double-check that it was made of wood, causing three more bugs to skitter out of her hollow eye socket. The captain shivered and quickly moved away.

"But this is impossible," Mike said as he moved around the hull. It must have been two hundred feet long, with three full masts and enough room on board for a crew of a hundred. Its timbers creaked mournfully with the breeze. "We're miles from the river, and half a continent from the ocean. How could something this enormous have ended up here?"

"Tides? Ice age? Aliens? All of the above?" the captain said.

"There's another one!" Dani called. She had reached the front of the pirate ship and was now running around its bow and out of sight.

"Dani! Wait!" Mike hurried after her, but he stopped short as he passed the front of the ship. His mouth dropped open.

It was a ship graveyard.

In the middle of the Amazon jungle.

The pirate ship, its front end wedged into the surrounding foliage, had obscured their view of a huge clearing that was dotted with sailboats, tugboats, even a British clipper ship lying on its side. But dwarfing them all was a full-size freighter, a cargo ship over 1,300 feet long, built to carry supplies all over the world. It was loaded with twenty-foot-long steel containers, the kind that fit on the back of a semitruck or a train car.

"Incredible," Aruna whispered.

Dani squealed like a ticklish dingo, unable to control herself as she scampered across the clearing, impulsively running from a rowboat to a fishing trawler and on to a weird little aquatic bus once used to take tourists from land to water and back again.

The air had the aroma of salt, fish, and decaying seaweed. It made the jungle around them smell like the ocean.

"These things shouldn't be here," Mike said with a weird little smile tugging at his mouth. "They can't be here."

"Long line of Shipwreckers in this world," the captain replied casually. "Just means we're headed in the right direction!"

The captain started to move on, but Mike stopped him.

"Wait, wait, wait," Mike said.

Dani turned, fully expecting to see Mike doing his best impression of a stick-in-the-mud again, stopping their adventure in its tracks. But she was shocked to find that he was grinning. His eyes were wide as he spun around, taking in everything that surrounded him. He was excited. For once, he was actually excited!

"This is amazing!" he cried. "I mean, number one, that Captain Kevin actually led us somewhere interesting—"

"Hey!" the captain protested.

"But, I mean, look at this. This is seriously a major discovery!"

He ran from one ship to another, pointing in disbelief.

"I mean, I've read about explorers who discovered a ship far from the ocean, but that was a single ship. One ship. This, this is dozens of ships! Incredible!"

Dani couldn't help smiling, too.

This was the Momo who had showed her how to climb a tree. The Momo who had taken her to her first superhero movie. The Momo who had bestowed upon her dog-eared copies of his favorite books, introducing her to the world of Bermuda Betty.

"And think of all the Shipwreckers who started their adventures right here!" Mike laughed. "Just like us!"

Dani grinned back at him.

"This really is amazing, Dani!" He ran up to his sister, literally hopping with excitement. "I didn't believe this was possible, but you were right. I think things are finally starting to turn around!"

Suddenly, there was a shard of lightning, then a crack of thunder. The sky opened up like a soggy piñata, dumping rain all over Mike's parade.

CHAPTER 20
THAT SHIP HAS SAILED

HERE'S THE THING about a rain forest: it's wet. According to the books Mike had devoured, fifty inches of rain a year was the minimum. The *minimum*. In a wet year, the skies could drop over five times that amount. Today, they were clearly hoping to break that record.

Mike and company were instantly soaked to the bone as buckets of water fell from the sky. Within minutes, streams of water slithered across the ground past them like liquid snakes.

"You didn't bring an umbrella in that backpack, did you?" Aruna asked Mike as they ran for shelter across the soggy field of ships.

"I wish." Mike wondered, not for the first time, if a backpack full of books was not the best thing to have in the jungle.

"There! That boat has a cover," Dani yelled.

Four pairs of feet splashed and sloshed through the mud, then onto the small schooner and the protection it offered from the downpour. It was not much of a boat—full of holes and listing slightly in the mud—but Mike was just grateful to be out of the rain.

"I'm soaked," Dani said.

"I'm drenched," Mike answered.

"I'm nauseous," the captain chimed in. He was holding his stomach, hunched over in discomfort. "Is anyone else feeling queasy?"

"I tried to stop you from eating that taco," Aruna countered.

"Oh, it's not that," Captain Kevin groaned, his face taking on a greenish hue. "I left all traces of that meal back on the *Roger Oberholtzer*, if you know what I mean."

Mike knew what he meant. He wished he didn't.

"I think it's land sickness," Captain Kevin moaned.

"What's land sickness?" Dani's brow was furrowed.

"It's the opposite of seasickness. Me, I'm at home on a boat, and I think I've been on land too long. Somebody find me a bush. *Gggggggh!*"

The captain bent over the railing of the boat and made the loudest retching noises that Mike had ever heard, like a gargling sea lion with a bullhorn.

But it was an entirely different kind of noise that caught Mike's attention.

"Wait, wait, wait," Mike said. "What's that?"

There's a particular noise that accompanies a landslide.

When the ground, saturated with water, can no longer maintain its stability, it rumbles downhill, ripping trees up by the roots, smashing through everything in its path. The earth roars.

Suddenly, a moving wall of water, mud, and debris

slammed into the back of the freighter. The enormous ship, already sitting atop a mixture of water and mud, had the perfect conditions to take a ride on nature's own Slip 'N Slide.

The mighty container ship moved. One hundred and ninety tons of solid steel began to slide impossibly across the land. It was headed directly toward the small schooner and the four humans standing on it with their mouths open.

"We're on land," Mike stammered. "Ships don't move on land." He'd read a lot of high seas adventures over the years, and he had yet to read about a freighter ship coasting across the jungle. They just didn't do that.

"Well, that one is," Dani said. "We gotta go!"

Captain Kevin, still leaning over the railing, was the first one to throw himself overboard, landing face-first in the mud. The others were right behind him, running for their lives.

"This isn't happening!" Mike screamed over the sounds of the pounding rain and the growling of the freighter cutting through the soaked soil.

"You wanted adventure?" Dani yelled. "This is adventure!"

The freighter smashed into the schooner, slicing through it like a gargantuan knife through a tiny pat of boat-shaped butter.

"*Ugghhhggggh,*" the captain said, running with one hand on his belly and the other over his mouth.

Mike risked a glance back at the approaching ship, its bow towering over them. The bottom of it, the portion dredging up gouts of mud and water, seemed to be covered in tiny jeweled barnacles. Their shiny jade coloring reminded Mike of something he'd seen before, but he couldn't remember what.

Right then he had other things on his mind, like literally running for his life.

"The rain stopped," Dani yelled.

"No," Mike said, looking up. "It's the ship."

Still on their heels, the high bow of the ship was now hanging over them, blocking the rain like a multiton steel umbrella.

The prow of the freighter chewing through the mud toward them was only thirty feet away.

"Faster!" Dani yelled. "Come on!"

The freighter was now twenty feet away.

"Keep going!" Mike yelled.

"Go, go, go!" Aruna screamed.

Ten feet away.

"Aaaagh!" Mike yelled.

"Aaaagh!" Dani yelled.

"Aaaagh!" Aruna yelled.

"Gggggg!" Captain Kevin made another retching noise.

"Over here," Mike hollered, pulling Dani to the side. Captain Kevin and Aruna followed his lead as he ran to the right of the massive ship.

He risked another look back and found that the ship was still directly behind them.

"The other way," Mike screamed. They all ran to the left this time, hoping to avoid the steel monster bearing down on them. But when Mike glanced over his shoulder, he was horrified to see the ship was still headed straight for them.

"It's like it's following us!" Dani cried.

"That's crazy!" said Mike. He refused to believe it.

But every time they ran left, the ship went left. Every time they ran to the right, the ship went to the right. It was like it had a mind of its own, crashing through rowboats and reducing sailing ships to rubble in its relentless pursuit.

"Maybe we need to stop!" Dani shouted.

"What? It'll crush us!" Mike hollered back.

"We can't outrun it," Aruna yelled.

"My gut says we stop. Take the risk!" Dani shouted. "We have to try!"

Mike thought it was insane. No, he *knew* it was insane. But he was out of ideas and they were out of time. Fighting every instinct in his body that was telling him to run, he forced himself to stop.

Aruna and Dani stopped beside him and a very nervous Captain Kevin joined them, standing a foot or so behind them, just in case.

The massive ship dug a ragged trench through the mud and dirt, still moving inexorably toward the very small, very exposed people.

Mike grabbed his sister's hand tightly. He closed his eyes and held his breath, his stomach clenching up like a fist.

The overwhelming noise of the splitting earth grew louder and closer . . . and then there was silence.

Mike opened his eyes.

He was staring at a bolt on the front edge of the ship's prow, two inches from his nose.

The freighter had come to a stop.

They stood in awe, almost afraid to say or do anything that might break the spell that was holding the ship in place.

And then Aruna laughed. To Mike, it sounded like a nervous guffaw, a release of built-up tension. But it was infectious, and soon Dani was laughing, too. Mike quickly joined in.

"I don't see what's so funny," the captain said, taking a step back from the hulking freighter looming over him. "That thing could've—"

The ship lurched another inch forward, cutting him off.

Captain Kevin screamed. And ran.

"No, no, no, no, no!" The others all yelled at him as one, begging him to stop, but he was already splashing across the clearing in a panic.

The ship moved.

Dani swore.

"We don't use those words," Mike yelled, grabbing his sister and running from the freighter.

"You're not the boss of me," Dani yelled back, her feet moving as fast as they could.

Aruna grabbed Mike and Dani by the arms and pulled them perpendicular to the direction of the ship, as Captain Kevin raced in the opposite direction.

The freighter slid past the kids, veering toward the fleeing captain, even as he bolted into the jungle. Its bow cleaved a new path through the trees, cutting them down like the world's largest ax. The ship finally slammed into an outcropping of rock and shuddered to a halt as the rain above petered out.

"That did not just happen," Mike said, putting his head between his legs to keep from hyperventilating.

"Where's Captain Kevin?" Dani asked, concern in her voice.

She got her answer a few seconds later as they ran around the back of the freighter to find the captain on the other side. He was alive. And he was screaming.

"It's here! The temple is here! The ship led us right to it!" The captain jumped like a giddy grasshopper. "We are so close now. I can feel it! Literally. My tummy's on fire! It wasn't land sickness. It was the jewel. It was the *jewel*!"

He lifted his shirt. His belly button was glowing green like Rudolph the Red-Nosed Reindeer on a snotty day.

Captain Kevin bounded into the dense jungle, leading the way. As always, he rambled on, commenting and making puns like his life depended on it. But as they reached the top of a small rise, Mike heard something besides the blathering boat captain.

"Quiet. Do you hear that?"

"Is it the blood pounding in my *temples*?" the captain said. "Or maybe—"

"No! Stop talking," Mike insisted. "It sounded like a plane."

Everyone stopped to look skyward and listen. Everyone except the captain.

"There! There it is!" he cried in excitement.

"The plane?" Dani asked.

"No. Nothing so *plain* as a plane," the captain laughed. "The temple. The temple! I found the *TEMPLLLLLLLLLLLLLE*!"

CHAPTER 21
NOW THE TEMPLE!

HALF SCREAMING AND HALF LAUGHING, Captain Kevin ran down the hill, leaping over roots and darting under tree branches.

Dani raced after him.

"I don't see anything." Mike scanned the area as he moved down the hill beside Aruna. "If this huge temple of his is around here, shouldn't we see it by now?"

All Mike could see was Captain Kevin in a clearing at the bottom of the valley, dancing with joy, flinging his arms in the air in celebration. He ripped off his pants and twirled them over his head.

"Are you allergic to pants?" Mike yelled.

"Maybe!" shouted the captain.

Mike frowned as he pushed through some foliage and finally saw the structure the captain was going crazy over. "That's not it, is it? It's tiny!"

Mike had been expecting something out of one of his adventure books, a colossal pyramid or an imposing ten-story structure like the South American version of an Aztec tomb. This was not that.

The "temple" was, at most, fifteen feet tall, no higher than the rooftop of an average one-story house; in some places, it was no taller than the captain. It looked tiny under the few towering trees around it, more like a scale model than a real Amazonian relic. It was vaguely pyramidal in shape, wider at the base and narrower at the top, with stone outcroppings that Mike thought could have been stairs, except for the fact that they weren't lined up in a row: one stair here, another over there, yet another around the back. A heavy stone statue sat at the top, squatting, expressionless and clearly bored. There were no windows or doorways, or any other obvious way to get in or out of the structure. To Mike, it looked like a garage-sized hunk of blocky modern art.

"This is it!" the captain cried, dancing his way back into his pants as the jewel in his gut glowed so brightly it could be seen through his shirt. "I found it! I am the greatest explorer in the history of history!"

"Are you sure this is it?" Mike asked. "I've seen Winnebagos bigger than this thing. . . ."

"Good things come in small packages, my lad," the captain laughed. "And this is certainly big enough to hold treasure. However, if my calculations are correct—"

"Doubtful," Aruna said under her breath.

"—then like the iceberg that sunk the *Titanic*, this is only the tip of the temple. The portion you see above the jungle floor is merely the highest spire of what should be a vast and mysterious labyrinth awaiting us beneath our feet."

"A hidden underground temple!" Dani said, joining the captain in his ridiculous dance of celebration. "That's awesome!"

Mike didn't want to admit it, but it actually was pretty awesome. Even though the structure *was* tiny, it still gave him butterflies in his stomach. Because it was a real temple. An actual, honest-to-goodness secret Amazonian temple! A relic of an ancient civilization sitting right in front of him. And the fact that it wasn't overflowing with tourists like Machu Picchu in Peru or Chichén Itzá in Mexico made it that much cooler. They were the only ones who were seeing this and, maybe, the only ones who had visited it in decades. This was something historians and archaeologists would kill to be a part of, Mike felt. They might even write books about it.

Mike tried to hide the smile that was creeping across his face, but it was no use. He was excited.

"So, what are we waiting for?" he asked, bouncing on the tips of his toes. "Let's go in!"

"Ah, that's the trick." The captain smiled with a gleam in his eye. "To find a way in. The great and glorious secrets of the Lost Temple of the Amazon will not be shown to every Dani, Aruna, and Momo who comes along."

"I've asked you not to call me that," Mike said, trying to maintain his excitement.

"And I've asked for a billion dollars and a date with a super-model, but that's not gonna happen, either," the captain replied, already turning his attention to the nearest wall of the temple. "These ancient structures always have a secret doorway or hidden panel, activated by just the right series of moves."

Captain Kevin pushed hard against a recessed area carved into the surface. He swiped his hand across the crevice between two stones, and then wiggled his butt against the base of the temple.

Nothing happened.

"Sometimes it's a combination of things," he went on, still confident. "Even voice commands can work."

He turned coyly away from the structure for a beat and then quickly swung around to face the temple, yelling out magic words.

"Open sesame!"

Nothing.

"Abracadabra!"

Nothing.

"Special delivery. Open the door!"

Nothing.

"Mom always said 'please' was the magic word," Dani volunteered.

"Please!" the captain implored.

Nothing.

Captain Kevin looked back at the others.

"Don't just stand there. Help."

Mike and Dani both leapt up to help, and Aruna rose slowly to join them.

Mike ran his hands along the surface of the temple wall. It was incredible. Every few feet there were strange symbols carved into the stone. Most were indecipherable markings from some long-dead language, but some were more like the hieroglyphics he had seen in books about Egypt. Of course, these weren't Egyptian, but they were characters carefully designed to represent things in the real world: A bird. A plant. A human skull. There seemed to be a lot of those.

Man, they're never going to believe this back home, Mike thought, setting his backpack of books down on the dusty ground. Right now, in this surreal moment, he didn't need to *read* about fictional heroes to get a rush of excitement. He was feeling that rush right now—in real life. He was the adventurer. Someone should be writing about *him*!

As the sun beat down on him from above, Mike pressed each bump and indentation on the off chance that it was a push-button trigger for some hidden passage. No luck. He heard Dani laughing and looked over to see Aruna lifting his sister up onto her shoulders so she could reach higher sections of the temple. He liked how they got along so well. If his sister had to idolize someone, better the strong Aruna than the less-than-admirable captain.

Mike circled the structure and found said less-than-admirable Captain Kevin doing a weird kind of dance across a temple ledge. The captain stomped one foot on a symbol before leaping to the next, like he was playing a bizarre game of hopscotch.

Without a doubt, Captain Kevin looked ridiculous. But for the first time since they'd met, Mike didn't immediately judge him for it. With all the strange things that had happened to them up to this point, who's to say this adventure didn't end with a weird Watusi dance atop an ancient underground temple?

Maybe this voyage hadn't all been the captain talking out of his *aft*. Maybe there really was a treasure after all.

Mike wasn't sure he believed it, not really. But he suddenly *wanted* to believe.

As he wiped the sweat from his forehead, a drop of perspiration hit the dry stone of the temple, momentarily darkening a spot on the thick layer of dirt coating the walls.

And it gave Mike a crazy idea about how they might get inside.

But before he could think it through, a whiny voice interrupted his revelation.

"I quit!"

It was Captain Kevin, yelling at the temple.

"This is hopeless!"

"What?" Mike was stunned, staring at the captain.

"It's impossible. There's no way to get inside this thing," the captain conceded. "This is a waste of time. You were right, Momo. Let's get out of here." Captain Kevin kicked the temple wall in disgust and turned to go.

"Are you kidding me?" Mike sputtered. "We just got here."

"And now we're leaving," the captain grumbled, adjusting his small pout to a full pout.

Mike had known several kids back home who gave up when they got one bad grade on a math test or struck out one time at bat, but this was crazy. Getting frustrated was one thing, but immediately throwing in the towel, and the entire adventure with it, was another.

"You dragged us all the way out here, and through

everything we've been through, just so you could give up and go home now?" Mike couldn't believe it.

"I didn't say *home*!" The twinkle was back in Captain Kevin's eyes. "I've heard stories about a sunken galleon in the North Atlantic off the coast of Bermuda. Worth millions. Billions, maybe. Of course, they say it's guarded by dinosaurs, but—"

"Stop!" Mike said. His head was spinning. Clearly, Captain Kevin had some kind of AADD, *adventure attention deficit disorder*, ready to give up one quest for another when things got hard. But Mike had come too far to give up now.

"We are not going to quit. We are going to get into this incredibly tiny temple if it's the last thing we do! Dani! Aruna! Come over here. I have an idea."

The four of them gathered together to hear Mike's plan, completely unaware of the mysterious eyes watching them from the jungle.

CHAPTER 22
MIKE'S WATERED-DOWN IDEA

"**WHAT IF WE USED WATER?**"

Dani, the captain, and Aruna were huddled around Mike beside the temple, trying to process what he'd just said.

"*What're* you talking about, Momo? The only thing all wet here is you and your idea," Captain Kevin chuckled.

"Did you read this in one of your books?" Aruna asked Mike, squinting at him skeptically.

"No, no. It just came to me."

Mike felt a sudden pang of uncertainty in his stomach as everyone stared at him, expectant, doubtful, and befuddled—in that order.

His self-doubt was quickly rising, making itself at home in his gut and riddling him with questions: What if his idea didn't work? What if it wasn't even possible? What if he looked like an idiot in front of everyone? Looking like an idiot had never stopped Captain Kevin from trying something, but Mike wasn't nearly as confident.

Back in fifth grade, Mike had stood up in front of his entire class and proposed a lunchtime book club. He thought it would be cool to get everyone reading the same exciting stories. Then they could talk about the cool parts and maybe even make up some stories of their own.

"And give up kickball?" Randy McCutchin had laughed from the back of the room. "You want to make us do even more reading than we already have to? What do you suggest for an encore? Extra pop quizzes?"

Everyone had laughed and Mike had sat down, never to risk making a bold suggestion in class again.

But now, faced with the possibility that Captain Kevin was about to give up on this escapade altogether, Mike tried to ignore the internal struggle churning in his stomach. *Maybe,* Mike thought, *my stomach isn't telling me this is a bad idea at all. Maybe my stomach is telling me this is a good one.*

Mike stood up straight, looked the others in the eyes, and went for it.

"Look, this temple was built hundreds if not thousands of years ago, right? Way before they had lasers and high-tech tools to make things airtight or watertight. So, if we pour water on the walls, it will find any tiny cracks that exist. It will trickle through and reveal where there's a moveable stone in the structure."

"The only cracks I see are the cracks in your plan," the captain laughed. "Now let me tell you all about Bermuda . . ."

"I think the water thing might actually work," Aruna said. "At least, it's worth a shot."

Mike beamed. He nodded at Aruna, appreciating her support more than he could say.

"Great," he said. "But it will take all of us. We just have to figure out how to get the water to the temple."

Dani pointed out some oversized fronds that they could use as makeshift water containers and the group quickly created a kind of bucket brigade, carrying rainwater from the muddy puddles on the ground to the temple. At Mike's instruction, they worked methodically, section by section, starting at the base of the temple with the idea that the most practical place for a door would be at ground level.

Each time they poured the water on the inclined temple wall, most of it would run right off to soak into the ground below, but some would trace the lines of the inscriptions and run along the indentations between adjoining stones. And each time Mike was hopeful that the water would uncover a more substantial division between building blocks and reveal a doorway. But each time he was disappointed.

"This idea of yours is dead in the water," complained the captain.

"Give it a chance," Dani said as she waddled to the temple, slopping more water out of her leafy container than she was keeping in it. "We still have one side left."

Mike splashed the remainder of his water on the temple. He watched it without much hope—maybe this idea hadn't been worth the risk of pitching after all. And then he froze in his tracks.

"Oh, my gosh."

"'Oh, my gosh,' what?" the captain groused. "Oh, my gosh, absolutely nothing happened just like every other time?"

"Oh, my gosh," Mike repeated, stunned. "It worked."

The captain leapt forward, pushing Mike out of the way with sudden renewed excitement.

"Where? Where? A door? Show me!"

It wasn't exactly a door, but it was a reaction—something had changed. Mike was sure of it.

"Aruna, hand me your water," he called out. She was by his side a second later, as was Dani, all of them watching Mike pour more water on a particular spot. A lot of it ran down the stone, making tiny, dirty rivulets on the surface. But a portion of the water seeped between two stones, disappearing between the rocks.

"What does that mean? Does that mean something?" Captain Kevin stammered, looking from Mike to Dani to Mike to Aruna and back to Mike. "What? What? What?"

"There's a gap," Mike said, trying to contain his excitement. "A gap that may be big enough so this rock can move."

"I knew it!" Captain Kevin screamed into the air. "Come on in, the water's fine!"

Mike felt a surge of pride rising from his troubled stomach, swelling up in his chest like a balloon. His idea was working. He had taken a risk—and it was actually working.

He grabbed a stick off the ground and dug into the crack between the stones, scraping out as much of the centuries-old dirt and moss as he could. Dani and Aruna quickly found their own sticks and did the same along the sides of the rock.

Captain Kevin watched eagerly as they worked to free it up as much as possible.

"Okay, on three," Mike said, "we all push as hard as we can on the rock, okay?"

"Wait! Push in or push out?" the captain asked.

"How do you push out?" Dani asked.

"Okay, never mind," the captain confirmed. "On three."

"One. Two. Three!" Mike called out.

Grunting and pushing and straining as one, they all threw their shoulders against the rock, digging their feet into the dirt to give it everything they had.

It didn't move.

"Crap." Captain Kevin slumped, disappointed. "There must still be a trigger or something that allows it to move. And that could be anywhere."

"Well, it's gotta be close," Dani said, still enthusiastic. "You wouldn't put the doorbell on the other side of the house, right?"

No one could argue with her keen architectural insight, so the foursome frantically pushed and pulled and poked and prodded every surface above, below, and beside the stone in question. Dani even popped her finger in her mouth and then wedged it into an oddly shaped indentation, giving the temple its first ever wet willy.

But it was only when all four of them pushed simultaneously on four distinct skull insignias on the ancient wall that they felt something shift.

The skulls clicked almost imperceptibly a few centimeters

back into the temple, and they heard the sound of two-thousand-year-old rock grinding against two-thousand-year-old rock as the stone blocking the entrance slowly sank into the ground.

"That's it!" Mike gasped, a surge of adrenaline coursing through him like lightning. "It took all of us!"

"Good thing we brought Aruna," Dani laughed, "or we never would have gotten in."

"*OhmyGod, ohmyGod, ohmyGod, ohmyGod,*" the captain stammered, his eyes growing larger and larger as the gap in the wall did the same.

"I can't believe it," Aruna said. "This is actually happening."

Mike's head flooded with images of every secret panel in every book he'd ever read. Now here he was, actually opening one in real life. He was amazed.

The top of the stone, a surface that hadn't seen the light of day in centuries, dropped down to the level of the ground and came to a stop. A small square hole, maybe two feet tall and two feet wide, led into the dark interior of the temple. They would have to squeeze to get in, but they had done it.

"WAHOOOOO!" Captain Kevin screamed, his voice echoing off the distant hills and scaring fifteen varieties of endangered birds into taking flight. "I DID IT!!!"

Aruna clapped Mike on the back, and Dani gave him a fierce hug. They knew who had done it. Score one for Mike Gonzalez.

Captain Kevin wriggled, making wild, happy, unintelligible noises of celebration.

"Waaaargaarah! We're goin' in, WAHHEYYHGGGHHKT—"

But the captain's rousing call was suddenly cut short by the blade of a sword pressed against his throat.

CHAPTER 23

THE GOONS STRIKE BACK

"**W**ELL, WELL, WELL,** if it isn't Big Nose."

Captain Kevin turned ever so slightly and found himself staring down the long, sharp swords of the two fine gentlemen whose map he had destroyed back at the taco shop.

Vincent stood smirking over the captain, his crisp white suit nearly glowing in the hot Brazilian sun. Rube looked the worse for wear, his clothes wrinkled from his time in the river and his arm painfully swollen from where the snake had bitten him.

"Why you always gotta be so rude?" Rube muttered, shaking his head at his partner.

"You may recall that we gave you the oh-so-appropriate appellation 'Big Nose' earlier," Vincent said, a hint of amusement in his droll English voice. "And now we find ourselves calling you that yet again. Big Nose."

The captain made his usual assortment of punny replies,

but Vincent ignored him, as Mike and many others had quickly learned to do.

"Deducing that your path would be determined by the river for the largest part of your journey, we quickly picked up your trail from the sky using a biplane that we . . . shall we say 'borrowed'?"

"I told you guys I heard a plane," Mike muttered.

"Well, that doesn't do us much good now, does it?" the captain said.

"But I told you a long time ago. Before we ever got to the temple!"

"Oh, great." The captain rolled his eyes. "Now you told them that we found the temple."

"We're literally standing on it," Mike yelled, his pulse surging.

"Whatever it takes to help you sleep at night," the captain said, shaking his head. "We all know what you did and didn't do."

Mike bit his tongue to keep from going postal.

Vincent continued as if he hadn't been interrupted. "Once you located the temple, it was child's play to find an appropriate landing area nearby so we could observe your efforts."

"Yeah, and then we waited in them bushes," Rube jumped in. "Nice and quiet like, no singing allowed, no pop songs or country tunes, not even a soft ballad to pass the time, even humming was a no-no—"

"Yes, we understand," Vincent interrupted, his disdain dripping like strawberry jelly from an overfilled PB&J. "You were a very good lad."

"Yeah, we watched quietly until you blokes figured out the way in—" Rube began.

"And now the treasure is ours," Vincent finished, giving the captain a sickly-sweet smile.

"No."

Vincent looked up to see who had spoken.

"No!" Mike strode up to the armed men, his eyes narrowed.

"What are you doing, Momo?" Dani tried to pull him back, but it was too late.

"No. This is a bunch of crap. You're not taking any treasure," insisted Mike.

"Excuse me?" Vincent sneered.

"It was my idea that opened it, and now you think you can just waltz in like . . . professional waltzers and take everything? No. It's not fair." Mike paced back and forth, waving his hands and yelling at the air. "You know what? I'm gonna close it! Ha! I opened it and I can close it! So there."

Vincent and Rube looked at the captain as if to say, *What's his deal?*

Captain Kevin shrugged. "He's been through a lot."

"My first win! It was my *first* win!" Mike was still ranting, hitting plants and kicking things out of his way like a toddler having a tantrum. "And the second I finally get invested in this ridiculous quest, WHAM! You guys think you can yank the rug out from under me!"

"Is 'wham' the right word?" Dani asked, scratching her head. "For a rug?"

"You know what dibs is?" Mike shouted, getting up in Rube's face. "This is *my* temple, and I called dibs!"

"He did, you know. He does have dibs. It was at least implied." Aruna nodded, unable to hide a small smile.

"The boy is right," Captain Kevin announced. "You've got no claim on this treasure or this temple. So, if you dare set one foot inside it, you are destined to become its next victim. The place is crawling with booby traps."

"Booby traps?" asked Rube, eyes darting back and forth nervously. "Did you say booby traps?"

"Enough," Vincent growled, clearly tired of the game.

"I'm telling you right now," Captain Kevin said, puffing out his chest, "the only way you'll get inside this temple is over my dead body."

"Well," Vincent said, pushing the sword harder against the captain's flesh, "now that the temple is open, I see no reason to keep you around, 'Captain.'"

"Whoa, whoa, whoa, let's not be hasty." Captain Kevin tried to backpedal. "You can't take what I say seriously. No one does! That was just bluster to look brave for the little girl."

"The little girl," Rube remembered. "The one what got the burning juice in me eyes? Where is she?"

Mike quickly swiveled around. He'd been so busy stomping around and yelling that he had lost track of her. Again. She was gone.

"Up here!" Dani called, a singsong tone in her voice.

They barely had time to register that Dani was atop the tiny temple before she shoved the heavy stone statue off the roof.

In a flash, dozens of disparate thoughts raced through Mike's brain. When had she left? Why hadn't he been watching her? How had she gotten up there without anyone seeing her? How much would it hurt to be crushed by a falling rock in the shape of a squat little statue? A lot? Or a whole *heckuva* lot?

The heavy stone statue bounced once on a ridge of the temple and then appeared to make a beeline for the three men below.

The captain, not surprisingly, used the distraction to save his own skin, diving backward away from the swords and rolling across the ground. Vincent was only a half-second slower, a half-second that almost cost him his life. He threw himself sideways, dropping his weapon and sliding painfully across the dirt on his hands and knees, ruining his fine white suit.

Rube was not so lucky. By the time he started to move out of the way, it was too late.

The heavy statue hit the ground inches from Rube, shattering into a million pieces of jagged shrapnel that flew in every direction. The largest piece, the size of a soccer ball, struck him in the leg, shattering his kneecap and knocking him off-balance. Smaller chunks cut his skin and pummeled his tattooed body like an angry hailstorm. Rube hit the ground, crying out in pain, and his sword skittered across the ground.

"Aaaugh, my leg!" Rube screamed.

"Aaaugh, my suit!" Vincent screamed as he saw the damage to his clothes. "Why is there so much dirt in this country?"

Yet despite his horrible loss, Vincent was the first to recover his senses and run for the nearest weapon. Without hesitation, Mike hurled his book bag at the older man, hitting him square in the gut, and Vincent folded like a paper airplane.

With Captain Kevin still curled up in a fetal position and Dani high atop the temple, Aruna was the closest to the discarded weapons, and she quickly scooped up both swords. Mike felt his hammering heart slow to a more reasonable tempo, and Captain Kevin leapt to his feet, his mouth firing faster than torpedoes.

"Yes! Yes! In your face! Who's got the big nose now, huh? Huh? You just got owned, my friend! And when I say 'my friend,' I'm saying it sarcastically, because you are not my friend. Not friends!"

The captain's arms flew over his head to "raise the roof" while his feet flailed like a spastic Riverdancer's. His lips, as usual, kept on flapping.

"Ladies and gentlemen, if you look to your left you'll see the lamest animal in the jungle, the white-bellied Vincenticus Defeaticus, and the stupid parasite who feeds on the carcasses that the larger animal leaves behind, Rubicus Legbusticus."

"Now who's being mean?" Rube groaned as he used both hands to try to hold his knee together.

"Oh, I haven't even started yet!" the captain laughed as he tap-danced back and forth, flitting between one fallen adversary and the other like a fickle hummingbird. "Sit back and relax, 'cause I'll be here all night! Try the veal! Tip your waitress!"

"Shut. Up."

It was Aruna, holding the sword against Captain Kevin's back.

"Okay, okay," he said, playfully holding up his hands.

"Maybe not my A-material, but certainly better insults than these two mouth breathers deserve, and I—"

"Shut! Up!" she yelled, digging the tip of the sword deeper. "For two days, I've had to listen to you run your mouth, day and night, night and day, bragging and lying and boasting and saying some of the stupidest things ever said by a human being on this planet. I can't take it anymore!"

And for one of the only times in his entire life, Captain Kevin shut up.

Mike, who had been helping Dani down from the temple, now turned toward the angry woman with the swords. Once again, he saw that it was up to the kids to clean up one of Captain Kevin's screwups.

"Look, Aruna, I understand," said Mike. "*Belieeeeve* me, I understand. There have been so many times I wanted to feed this moron to the piranhas, or shove him under a freighter ship, or sacrifice him to the caimans, or slip up beside him while he was sleeping and—"

"I think she gets the idea, Momo," Dani interrupted gently.

"The point is, we all kind of hate him," Mike insisted. "Seriously. Show of hands. Who hates him?"

Vincent's hand shot up to join Mike's. Aruna pulled one sword away to raise her hand. Even Rube, so worried about insulting others, took one hand away from his swollen knee-cap to raise it over his head. Only Dani kept both hands down.

"But despite that, he's not the enemy," Mike went on. "And right now, that's what we have to stay focused on. The enemy."

Aruna took a deep breath and then let it out slowly.

"You're right," she said quietly, before turning to address the thugs. "Vincent. Rube. On your feet."

Vincent stood and helped his cohort to his feet. Rube winced at the pain, but with his partner's support, he hobbled over to stand beside Aruna.

"Yes, boss." Rube grimaced.

Smiling, Aruna turned her swords back on Captain Kevin.

"Wait," Dani said, confused. "Why did he call you 'boss'?"

"Oh, that's easy, sweetie." Aruna smiled. "Because they work for me."

FROM THE JOURNAL OF CAPTAIN
KEVIN ADVENTURESON

The Shipwrecker's Code.

It's the code of the Shipwreckers.

And I was going to inscribe its unchanging, infallible rules right here for all time, but then I realized I wanted to add something to it.

Remember when I said, "Never trust anyone"?

Well, *lemme* tell you, I was right, and it's a big responsibility being right all the time.

But now I want to amend that from "never trust anyone" to "never ever trust anyone." *Ever*, ever. Even if you're already not trusting them, definitely "not trust" them more than you were even "not trusting" them before.

Besides loyalty and *courageousnessity*, I'd say the number one thing in the Shipwrecker's Code should be the "not trusting" thing. And the number one thing *after* "never trust anyone" —so this would be the *second* number one thing—is never trust someone named Aruna.

Someday, if you become a Shipwrecker, you will

live the code. And all its secrets will finally be revealed to you.

But in the meantime, trust no one, trust no one named Aruna, and—trust everything I say, because I am your captain.

I got this.

CHAPTER 24
BETRAYED

DANI STARED UP AT ARUNA and felt something inside her shrivel.

Over the last two days, she had really grown to like Aruna, to admire her, and had even wanted to *be* like her. They had become friends, hadn't they?

Was it all a lie?

"Wait. I'm confused," Captain Kevin said, surprising no one. "What do you mean they work for you? Like, you hired them to help you dig a ditch or move boxes to a new apartment or something? Is Vincent secretly a notary? I'm not following."

Aruna reached out and hit the captain in the chest.

"No, you moron. I am their boss," Aruna explained. "They work for me. I am the mastermind of this little gang of thieves, all put together to swindle you out of the treasure."

"Ahhhh," the captain said, nodding. Then he paused. "Nope, still not getting it."

Aruna smacked him again and placed the sharp tip of her sword against his throat.

Captain Kevin put his arms up.

"Hey, hey, hey. No need to turn me into a shish kebob. Or, technically, a shish ke-*kevin*."

"Why?" Mike asked Aruna. "I don't understand. Why have you been trying to fool us this entire time? Why didn't you reveal yourself at the taco shop? Or on the boat? Or in the jungle? Or literally at any number of other times I could list?"

"Well, that certainly would have been easier," she agreed. "But there was a bit of an unexpected complication. You two."

She looked over at Dani, who quickly looked away.

"I'm not listening to you," said Dani, folding her arms defiantly. "Probably just more lying liar lies!"

Aruna cleared her throat and turned to Mike.

"If you must know, the original plan was to find out what Captain Kevin knew, take his jewel, and steal his boat," Aruna explained. "We weren't planning on the fact that he was babysitting kids."

"Yes, you filthy little urchins fouled everything up," Vincent snarled.

"Again with the insults," Rube groaned.

"So, I decided to bide my time until I could figure out what your relationship was with the captain," said Aruna. "And how best to turn it to my advantage."

Dani suddenly remembered when Aruna had asked her about just that. Was that what this woman had been doing the entire time? Quizzing her for information? Dani somehow felt worse than sad. She felt used. Aruna had been playing them from the moment they'd met.

"And as the time passed," Aruna continued, "I realized that I could use the captain as my tool. By letting him take the lead, he suffered the brunt of all the obstacles in our way, while I sat back and enjoyed the show."

Her smile quickly faded.

"Unfortunately, he is so ill-equipped to do anything at all, he nearly got us killed in the process. Multiple times."

Mike applauded her slowly and sarcastically. "Congratulations. It really requires a lot of skill to fool an idiotic man, a preteen boy, and a little girl. Your parents must be so proud."

"Oh, grow up," Aruna shot back. "I told you, you weren't supposed to be part of this. You were in the wrong place at the wrong time, that's all."

"I hate you," spat Dani.

Deep down, she wasn't sure if *hate* was the right word. She was still confused. But whatever was coursing through Dani made her brow furrow and her hands clench.

Aruna leaned down to look Dani in the eyes.

"Let's not forget, there is a lot of money at stake here. A lot. Like château-in-France money, and I don't even like France. So, I'm not about to throw it all away because a little girl got her feelings hurt."

The icy coldness in Dani's stomach suddenly boiled over and she erupted like a four-foot-tall volcano. She shoved the cruel woman back as hard as she could.

Aruna was so shocked that she simply stared at Dani, her mouth hanging open. It was only for a second, but that second was all that Mike and the captain needed.

Captain Kevin kicked Rube in the bad knee. The heavyset

man screamed in agony and fell back, toppling into his taller companion.

"Watch out, you ninny!" Vincent yelled. "You're getting your blood on my suit!"

At the same time, Mike lunged for Aruna, aiming low. Her legs buckled and she landed hard on her back, knocking the wind out of her. One sword went flying, skittering across the ground. She was able to hold on to the other one and quickly scrambled back to her feet.

The captain lunged for the fallen weapon. Aruna swung the other sword up at his head, barely missing and slicing off a chunk of the matted hair sticking out of his ball cap.

For Dani, time seemed to freeze. Aruna had nearly cut off Captain Kevin's head.

Even if Aruna had lied to them, did that mean she was really willing to harm Captain Kevin? Dani didn't want anyone to get hurt—the thought made her feel queasy. But she couldn't just stand here and hope that everything would work out okay.

"Captain!" Dani cried. She scooped up the fallen sword and threw it in a high arc over Aruna's head.

And somehow, some way, in a move that defied all expectations, Captain Kevin actually caught the sword.

"Ha!" he cried. "I caught it!"

"Now use it!" shouted Dani.

Steel met steel as Aruna and Captain Kevin clashed swords.

Aruna lashed out again and again, aggressively swinging for blood, but Dani was impressed as the captain managed to repel each blow, whipping his blade as fast as he possibly could.

Captain Kevin was equally impressed with Aruna. "You fight really well for a waitress."

"I'm not a waitress, you moron," she said. "You honestly don't remember me, do you?"

"Ohhhh." He smiled knowingly even as he defended himself against her rapidly increasing attacks. "Look, lady, I don't know what kind of romantic notions you cooked up in that little head of yours, but I'm not looking for anything serious."

She lunged at him and their swords locked.

"We did NOT have a 'relationship,' you pig."

With a flourish, Aruna whipped off a thick blond wig with her free hand to reveal her straight brown hair hidden beneath it.

Slowly, a look of recognition came over the captain's face. Then, just as quickly, it disappeared.

"Nope. Still don't know you."

She growled in her fury, yanking her sword away from his long enough to bring the hilt down on his head.

Dani winced as the sword clanged against his skull like a gong.

"You ruined my life! And you don't even remember!"

"Okay, you're going to have to be a bit more specific," said the captain, whipping his sword up to deflect the next attack. "I've ruined a lot of lives."

"Egypt. The Nile. Five years ago."

"Ahhh, yes," he remembered, smiling. "That was an amazing shipwreck."

"I had a different name back then—I was a different person, really. But you came along and convinced me that I could leave that life behind by helping you steal a jewel from a ship called the *Egyptian Queen*."

"Good plan." The captain nodded.

"But you sank the boat! With me still on it!" she yelled, slashing her sword at him in an angry blur. "I was trapped below deck—about to die—while you were racing away with a ruby the size of your fist."

"Ohhhhh! Now *that* I remember!" The captain grinned.

"And earlier today," she wailed, "you sank another boat! With me on it! Again! I vowed to do whatever it took to get my revenge. Against this dummy." She clocked him again with the butt of her sword.

"So, wait," Mike said. "So you changed your name and left your old life behind, became an adventurer, hired goons, laid a trap—all of it—just to get back at . . . this dummy?"

"It does sound a bit silly when you say it out loud," Rube whispered.

Aruna snarled and lashed out at the captain with renewed fury.

Dani felt stuck, staring at the two people she had grown so close to in the last forty-eight hours, now at each other's throats. She was watching her heroes fight: Bermuda Betty battling it out with Captain Kevin. She couldn't bear it.

"Don't hurt him!" Dani yelled. "And don't hurt her, either!"

Aruna pushed the captain back, sword clattering against sword again and again. Amazingly, Captain Kevin countered her every blow and grew even cockier than usual.

"Now folks, if you look to your right," Captain Kevin narrated, "you'll see my sword."

"Shut up," Aruna yelled.

"And if you look to the left," the captain continued, "you'll also see my sword."

"Shut up!" Aruna yelled again.

"And if you look behind me—" Captain Kevin started. But he wasn't able to finish. Vincent had snuck up behind him, breathing down his neck and ready to brain him with a large rock.

"No!" Dani cried. She didn't stop to think. She acted.

She slammed into Vincent from behind, throwing her body against the backs of his knees. His legs bent against his will and he lost his balance, the rock above his head crashing down with him.

When Vincent finally looked up, Dani gasped, her hands flying to her mouth.

His nose was gone.

"Momo! I broke his face!" she cried fearfully.

"*Wod* are you *dalking aboud*?" Vincent said dully, his already nasal voice sounding as if he had contracted a serious head cold.

"I knocked him over and the rock cut off his nose!" Dani squealed, feeling horrible about what she'd done. "It's so gross!"

"But there's no blood," Mike said, running up beside her.

Vincent's hands flew to his face and he could feel the absence of a nose where a nose most certainly should be.

"You *idiods*!" he growled. "Where *id by dose*?!"

"Super gross," Dani said as she spotted the missing piece in a patch of grass. It looked like a flesh-colored cockroach.

She grabbed a twig to spear the nose and lifted it up by the nostril.

"If you *bust dow,* by real *dose* was *cud* off *id* a sword *fighd bady* years ago," he muttered as he grabbed the artificial schnoz from Dani and attempted to affix it back onto his face.

"Ha!" Captain Kevin yelled from across the temple. "I guess we won by a nose!"

"*Veddy fuddy.*" Vincent scowled.

"Oh, don't get your nose out of joint," the captain continued, clearly enjoying himself. "I don't mean to rub your nose in it. You'll have that thing back on in *nose* time."

"Stop making puns!" yelled Aruna, lunging back into her sword fight with the captain.

"Okay, now Captain Kevin's the one being rude," Rube said from his spot leaning against the temple. "See what you started?"

Vincent ignored him and turned his back on the others. He huffed with frustration as he tried to attach his prosthetic proboscis in private.

"Hey, kids, Vincent is the only guy here who actually paid money to pick his nose," the captain joked, still countering every one of Aruna's moves with one of his own.

"As far as you *nose,*" Dani added.

"Ha! That's my girl!" the captain laughed.

"Okay, *dat's* enough!" Vincent roared, one hand holding his fake beak in place. "I'm serious. We're done."

He plopped down beside Rube at the side of the temple.

"You ruined my suit, my *good* suit, and now you knock off my nose and see fit to mock me for it, cruelly and incessantly?

Well, that is where I draw the line, sir. We are not getting compensated enough for this amount of abuse. We quit!" Vincent slammed his fist down beside him, accidentally triggering a pressure-sensitive stone.

Instantly the ground gave way beneath them as a trapdoor dropped open and the two men plummeted into darkness. Their screams echoed off the walls of what appeared to be a bottomless pit.

"Oh," said Captain Kevin. "There's the booby trap."

No one heard them hit bottom, if they ever did. It was only when the trapdoor lifted itself back into place that the sound of their screaming was finally cut off.

Dani's breath caught in her throat. She stared, wide-eyed, at the spot where the two men had been sitting. It was as if they'd disappeared off the face of the earth. She'd known all along that this trip might be a little dangerous, but she never believed that anyone would really get hurt. For the first time, she began to wonder if all this was worth it.

The clatter of a sword hitting the ground redirected Dani's attention.

The captain had finally lost his weapon, and Aruna was holding her sword to his throat. The battle was over.

"Well, then," Aruna said through clenched teeth, "I think we're done here. And it looks like I won't have to split the jewels three ways anymore, will I?"

Dani couldn't believe how cold she sounded.

The woman motioned toward the temple opening, waving her sword like a malevolent tour guide.

"So . . . shall we go inside?"

CHAPTER 25
THE BELLY OF THE BEAST

THEY WADED SLOWLY into the darkness, crawling like little babies into a playpen of doom.

Holding makeshift torches to light their way, the foursome entered the temple on their hands and knees; Mike was first, keeping Dani right behind him, followed by the captain, so Aruna could keep her eye on him as she brought up the rear.

"Ouchie," Dani cried to the captain. "You're burning my butt."

"Whoops. Don't want any hot crossed buns," Captain Kevin said as he lowered his torch and eased back a bit.

One by one they reached a large interior room and stood. It was a good ten degrees cooler, and the air was stale, the smells of mildew and dust filling Dani's nose and mouth. She wrinkled up her face. Hadn't anybody thought to put a window in this place? Or maybe an air freshener?

The chamber was small—the size of a bedroom—with thick stone walls and a low oppressive ceiling. But the most striking feature protruded from the wall on the far end: a massive carved reptilian mouth—half snake, half caiman, all teeth—like the head of a giant ready to strike, but frozen in stone.

To Dani, the statue seemed to move in the flickering light of the torches. She drew closer. The reflective gems in its eyes glinted, while the dark recesses of its throat swallowed up the light. A foul-smelling wind blew out of the snake's yawning jaws, twisting around Dani and causing the flame on her torch to sputter and dance. A shiver ran down her spine.

"Over here," called Aruna, breaking the silence. Dani hadn't realized how deathly quiet this room seemed after the noisy drone of the jungle and its creatures. She happily moved away from the creepy snake head to join the group once more.

"The glyphs on the walls, they tell the story of this temple," Aruna said, pointing at the unusual markings. She was talking quickly now, clearly geeking out. "They tell how and why it was built: to house a kind of mystic focal area. We are standing in a very powerful geographical nexus point."

"I'm still mad at you," Dani replied. But her curiosity temporarily overwhelmed her anger. "So, what does that mean?"

"It means that she's been drinking too much of the local Kool-Aid," the captain said, rolling his eyes.

Aruna poked the captain with the sword.

"Ow," he said.

"Look at these symbols." Aruna eagerly brushed the dirt away from a section of the wall. "A ship. A triangle. A twister, like a tornado or whirlpool. And finally, a pyramid with only the tip appearing above the ground."

"That last one—that's this place, right?" Dani asked.

"Exactly," Aruna replied. "And if I'm reading these correctly, they reference great ships trapped in a mysterious triangle and transported through a portal to end up . . . here."

She let the thought hang in the air like a balloon that no one would touch, afraid of popping it. Mike finally broke the silence.

"The Bermuda Triangle?" he asked. "Those ships we passed are from the Bermuda Triangle?"

"How else could they have gotten here?" Aruna asked, caught up in the moment. "Look, for decades scientists have theorized about wormholes in space and paths between dimensions. Who's to say that unexplained phenomena on Earth aren't the same thing?"

"Like those upside-down trees," added Dani. "And all that static electricity in the jungle!"

"Hold on," Mike interrupted. "So you're saying that the people who carved these two thousand years ago knew all this?" Mike said. "Hundreds of years before those ships were even invented?"

"Yes!" Aruna nodded. "There are strange forces at work here, things that man does not understand. Certainly not this man." She jerked her head toward the captain.

Dani took a closer look at the drawings that had inspired Aruna's theory. A ship. A triangle. A twister. And a buried pyramid. Aruna's interpretation did make some sense. But what about the fifth image—the one of the pyramid floating above the ground? She hadn't mentioned that one.

"So, what's this symbol mean?" Dani asked.

"Enough with the language lecture," Captain Kevin

groaned. "I signed up for a treasure hunt, not *Archaeology For Dummies*."

"You have no idea what you're dealing with, do you?" Aruna shook her head sadly. "The jewels in this temple are far more valuable than any price you could get by selling them. Your glowing, distended abdomen is proof that these stones have special properties and powers."

"Seriously?" Mike frowned. "Hold on. I feel like we're in Bigfoot territory again here. Although, with what we've been through lately, I may not be as skeptical as I used to be."

Dani spoke up. "The captain was right about the temple and he was right about the jewel . . . at least the one in his belly. Maybe the rest of it is true, too."

"Like the powers and the mummies and stuff?" asked Mike.

The captain shrugged. "Sure. Why not?"

Aruna stepped over to another wall of pictograms, running her fingers over their ancient shapes and symbols.

"I don't know for sure what's down here, but I've searched for these stones for a very long time," Aruna said with conviction. "No one knows the extent of their powers. But I intend to find out. They may have influence over life and death itself."

"You believe what you want, Mystic Mary," the captain mocked Aruna as he strode across the room. "But when your shiny crystals don't bring you a flying carpet and a goose that lays magic beans, don't come crying to me."

"Okay, don't start fighting again," Dani pleaded. "We don't even have any jewels here to fight over yet."

"Well, not the bulk of the treasure, that's for sure," Aruna confirmed. "But there are one or two jewels. And we're going to leave 'em right where they are, aren't we, Captain?"

She hadn't even turned to look, but she knew that Captain Kevin was about to pry the gems from the stone reptile's glittering eyes.

"But they're just waiting to be taken," he whined.

"Exactly. They're a trap for every rube that walks in here. Save your effort for the treasure trove waiting for us down below."

"I don't know," Dani said, looking from the jewels to the captain. "I'm not sure we should be taking anything at all from here."

"Aw, don't let Aruna's spooky stories spoil your adventure," Captain Kevin said. "She's already ruining mine with that pointy sword."

"No, it's not that." Dani frowned. "The jewels aren't ours. The stuff in this temple doesn't belong to us. I wouldn't go into somebody's house back where we live and take something from them. So what makes it okay to do it here?"

Dani saw her brother smiling at her. She could tell he agreed with her.

"Uh, hello?" the captain chuckled. "What part of 'treasure hunt' didn't you understand, missy?"

"I liked the hunt," she agreed. "The quest part was fun, but if we're really going to take things from this place, that's just stealing."

"Exactly." Aruna nodded. "And that's precisely why we're here. To steal. So, less moralizing, and more moving. Let's go."

She gestured for Dani and Mike to join the captain at the snake's mouth.

"Wait, are you saying that's a doorway?" Dani said.

"I knew that," Captain Kevin said quickly.

Dani reluctantly stepped toward the mouth, but her brother quickly grabbed her shoulder, stopping her so that he could go first—always protecting her, even when she didn't need it.

Moving slowly, heads down, they stepped between the stone fangs and onto the beast's rocky tongue.

"Don't touch anything," Mike whispered to Dani as he edged forward into the constricting throat of the stone creature. "And put your feet on the same spots that I do."

"Oh, right. Like one wrong step and the whole place will blow up," the captain laughed. "Somebody's read one too many books and seen one too many movies. It's *Momo Gonzalez and the Temple of Boom*!"

To prove his point, the captain reached back to grab hold of one of the fangs.

"It's just an old rock carving."

Then the fang shifted in his hand.

"MOVE!" Aruna screamed, shoving him into the kids, using her body weight to propel them all forward.

The upper jaw of the carving crashed down behind them. The huge stone shattered, sending up a cloud of choking debris. The noise was deafening. For a moment, they couldn't see or hear anything.

Eventually, the dust cleared and the ringing in their ears abated.

Dani looked up and found herself in another world.

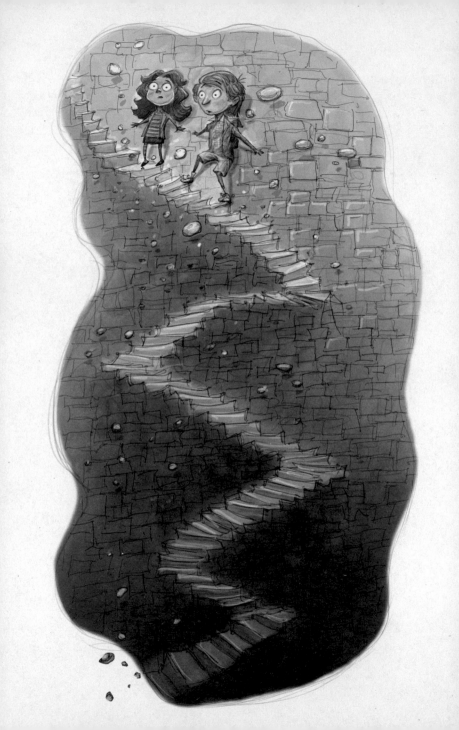

CHAPTER 26
THE DARK SECRET TEMPLE OF SECRETIVE SECRET DARKNESS

MIKE LOOKED ACROSS a vast chamber that spread out below them, built deep into the earth itself. Ancient stone stairwells clung to the walls, spiraling far down into the impenetrable darkness. It was overwhelming.

"Told you it was like an iceberg," Captain Kevin said. "But without all the ice."

Mike glanced behind him. The reptile throat had collapsed, cutting off any chance of turning back.

His sister, of course, wasn't thinking about turning back. Her distaste for stealing had been momentarily steamrolled by the thrill of discovery. She ran to the top of the staircase, leaning out to get a better look. Mike grabbed the collar of her shirt, yanking her back as several stones gave way beneath her feet and plummeted into the darkness. He waited breathlessly to hear the rocks hit bottom. They never did.

"It's a bit of a fixer-upper," Captain Kevin joked. "Good bones, though."

Mike stared over the edge, eyes wide.

They were peering down into an underground pyramid from its highest point, buried beneath thousands of tons of earth.

Mike couldn't help thinking of all the haunted houses he'd read about, with walls that dripped blood, or all the decrepit castles occupied by spirits of years gone by. One or two of the books had been so scary that he couldn't read them in bed without having nightmares. But *reading* about creepy places and actually being in one were two entirely different things.

Mike hugged himself without even realizing it. He stole another glance into the impenetrable darkness below.

"I don't suppose there's any chance that they left your treasure on the top floor?" Mike asked without much hope.

"I think it's under there," the captain said vaguely.

"Under where?" Dani asked.

"Ha! I made you say '*underwear*'!" the captain laughed.

"The jewels are going to be down deep," Aruna said. "In nearly every civilization, from the Mayans to the Aztecs to the Egyptians, they reserved the deepest, most protected level for the burial chamber and the treasures that would accompany the departed to the next world."

Mike raised his eyebrows at her.

"You're not the only one who's read a book," said Aruna. "Now let's get going. Move." She jabbed at Captain Kevin with her sword.

"You know, you were a lot nicer when you were wearing the wig," Captain Kevin pouted as he headed for the stairs.

Mike took the lead again, stepping through a curtain of spiderwebs and onto the stone stairs that encircled the chamber. The orange flame flickered at the end of his torch, licking the walls with pulsing light. He gave one last look back at the thin shards of daylight leaking in above them and wondered if they would ever see the sun again.

The odds of that didn't seem very high, but maybe there was something he could do to improve them.

Reluctantly, he reached into his bag and pulled out one of his books. Gritting his teeth and closing his eyes, he opened the cover. Fighting his instincts, he tore out one of the pages.

"Momo!" Dani grabbed his arm. "What are you doing?"

"Leaving a trail," he said, his voice low as he dropped the first page on the ground and willed himself to rip out another. "Just in case."

They descended from one level to the next, from one tier to another, ever deeper into the dark earth. At each successive level, there were more and more passages leading away from the main stairway. The lower they went, the larger the space, with more opportunities for hidden rooms, alternate passages, and undiscovered mysteries.

Mike could see that Dani's initial excitement over the temple had waned. He thought about taking his sister's hand to comfort her, but he didn't. He was too busy scanning the darkness for whatever might lurk within while continuing to litter the ground with bits of paper.

"Look," Aruna said, "I know this is rough, but I already told you, you kids weren't supposed to be here. I tried to get rid of you guys. I even let Mike turn the boat around to get you back to your parents."

Dani's only response was to clomp even more sullenly down the stairs.

"Fine, whatever," Aruna said. "You don't have to like me. Just bear with me for the next thirty minutes and you'll never have to see me again."

"Because you're gonna kill us." Dani scowled. "Right?"

"No, I'm not going to kill you," responded Aruna, who actually sounded shocked. "Why would I kill you?"

"Oh, good," Captain Kevin sighed.

"Oh, I'd kill *you*," Aruna clarified to the captain. "I'd kill you in a heartbeat."

Mike normally would have smiled at the startled look on Captain Kevin's face. But there was nothing funny in this place.

The lower they went, the more oppressive it felt. Mike's breathing was shallow now, his eyes darting nervously around the shadowy interior. He took smaller, more tentative steps, his nerves on edge. He jumped at every small sound. Something about the place seemed . . . wrong. Mike couldn't put it into words, but he knew they shouldn't be here. This was not a place for the living. This was a tomb for the dead.

Not that he believed what Aruna and the captain had said about curses and undead creatures. That was ridiculous. But it was much harder to be rational when it felt like the darkness was creeping in from all sides.

Adventure or not, he would have turned around and found a way out if he wasn't being taken down at sword point. The only people in stories who ventured foolishly into dark foreboding tombs were the ones who never came out alive.

The stairs finally, thankfully, ended at a small landing with a stone bridge, which hovered above the vast emptiness and stretched to the opposite side of the temple. The bridge was bookended by two rough-hewn columns mounted with matching statues of snarling panthers. But where the panthers' faces should have been were human skulls.

This is real, Mike thought. *This is not a theme park or a tourist trap. This is real.*

He stopped. Better safe than sorry.

"What's the holdup, Chicken Little?" the captain asked.

Mike searched the surrounding area and soon found a loose stone, wiggling it out of its position in the wall.

"What's that for?" Dani asked.

"Looking before we leap." Mike tossed the stone out onto the center of the bridge.

Instantly, the entire bridge collapsed like it was made of Popsicle sticks, plummeting down into the abyss. The four of them stared, mouths open, knowing it easily could have been them.

"Where are my manners?" the captain said, backing up a step and gesturing to Aruna. "Ladies first."

Aruna glowered.

"So, what do we do now, Captain?" Dani asked, staring at the yawning gap in the path.

"Onward and forward and crossword and free bird," the

captain said, patting his stomach and the jewel it held, before striding up to the sheer edge of the landing.

"Okay, that's a long drop," Mike warned. "Maybe we should stop and think about this for a second."

"There's no time for thinking when your life is an adventure!" the captain explained. He yanked on a length of vine that snaked down from a beam high above them. He pulled twice to check that it was taut and then, without hesitation, he leapt, swinging over the abyss.

Mike wasn't sure what the captain thought would happen. Maybe it was something Captain Kevin had seen in his years of watching more successful adventurers in the movies. But whatever it was, it didn't happen.

The vine snapped.

And the captain plummeted into the darkness below.

CHAPTER 27
IF THESE WALLS COULD TALK

TO THE CAPTAIN'S CREDIT, he only screamed for a few seconds.

And then his body hit solid rock.

Dani flinched at the sound it made.

"Are you okay?" she yelled, peering over the edge to try to see him in the darkness below.

The only answer was a weak, distant groan, like the sound a dying walrus might make.

"Hang on. We'll be right there!" she called.

It took several minutes to find another way down. The air was even colder here—and Dani found it hard to breathe.

Each level of the temple they reached was larger than the one above it, and this floor was no exception. This chamber was massive, a cathedral of darkness. Dani kept waiting for her eyes to adjust, but there were still parts of the room so cloaked in shadows that she could barely see a thing. It was as if the blackness went on forever, like they weren't underground but in the vast emptiness of space.

227

What they *could* see was the nearest wall, lined with intricately decorated containers for the dead.

But Dani didn't care about that. She was searching for the captain. She moved through the gloom, passing one dark object after another, feeling her way along.

Suddenly, something beside her groaned and grabbed her wrist.

Dani screamed.

"My tummy hurts," the groaning figure said weakly.

It was the captain, lying on a stone slab.

Dani started breathing again.

"If your tummy hurts, that means we're in the right place!" Aruna said, already pushing past him with her torch. She moved into the darkness slowly, carefully, until she found what she was looking for.

Bending down, she touched her torch to the remains of a funeral pyre, a conflagration of half-burned wood from centuries ago.

The brittle remains quickly ignited, creating a small bonfire in the center of the chamber. Then the fire spread, thin branches of flame extending out in four directions at once.

"Uh-oh," Dani said.

With the light of the fire, however, they could now see indentations in the rock floor—almost like gutters, but filled with what must have been some sort of slow-burning oil. It acted as a path for the flame, spreading light and warmth to the four corners of the room, where golden braziers atop engraved pedestals burst to life with crackling flashes of yellow and orange.

"Let there be light," the captain groaned, slowly getting up.

This system for central lighting and heating from ancient times gone by was quick, effective, and impressive. For the first time since entering the structure, they could finally see the details of the temple in all their glory.

Dani was blown away. The chamber was enormous—a rectangular room easily as large as a football field. But instead of white chalk every ten yards, the markings here were stone coffins radiating out from the walls. They all seemed to be pointing to a massive structure against the far wall, where two immense statues kneeled on either side of a large tomb. Their bodies had human forms, but animal heads: a snake and a jaguar, respectively. Though kneeling, they also appeared ready to leap to the defense of the sacred tomb they guarded.

"No, no, don't get up," the captain told the statues as he limped across the room.

The tomb between the figures was striking, and it bore more than a passing resemblance to the top of the temple. But unlike the exposed portion aboveground, this structure had a very clear entrance, surrounded by more cryptic symbols and blocked by a towering slab of granite.

As the others followed Captain Kevin, Dani admitted to herself that she was now more than a little spooked. Her footsteps echoed off the walls of the vast chamber, giving Dani the feeling that they were being followed.

She quickened her pace to catch up to her brother, who was sniffing at what looked like tall candleholders rising from a stone foundation. He craned his neck to look up at the vaulted ceiling, an imposing collection of stalactites high overhead. To Dani, they looked like the dripping fingers of some giant monster reaching down to grab them. Normally, she would have thought this was totally cool, but now it just seemed creepy.

Suddenly, the captain lurched. It looked as though something had grabbed his belt buckle and yanked him forward.

"Whoa, whoa, whoa!" he cried, his hands grabbing his stomach. "I think the baby kicked."

"What?" Dani asked, confused.

"The jewel," he answered. "It's hip-hopping like a jumping bean."

Dani moved toward the captain and patted his tummy. The jewel was actually moving.

Slowly, he tried to follow the movements of the gem in his gut.

"Warm. Warm. Warmer," he said as his intestines steered him across the room. "Cold. Colder. Ice Station Zero."

Dani knew this game and helped turn the captain in the opposite direction.

"Warmer. *Warmerrrrr*," he said. "Hot. Red hot! I'm on fire!"

He stopped right in front of the large tomb between the two kneeling figures. And belched.

"Right here," he said authoritatively. "I've got a gut feeling about this."

"You seriously believe your abdomen is a compass pointing to the jewels?" Mike asked. "Which is a sentence that no human being has ever said before."

"Maybe," the captain said, "but you know what they say: 'No guts, no glory!'"

The four of them stared at the towering granite slab that blocked the entrance.

"Now what?" Dani asked. "How do we get in? More water?"

She looked at her brother expectantly.

"Not much of that down here," Mike said. "But I'd bet you anything that we need to do something with that jewel." He pointed at Captain Kevin's belly, which was shaking like a bowlful of jelly.

Dani looked away from the door at the disturbing carvings around it.

"Here. I can cut the jewel out right now." Aruna stepped toward the captain, sword extended like a giant scalpel.

"Whoa, no . . . hey, ho, hold the phone," Captain Kevin babbled, backing away. "There's gotta be a way to get the treasure where I don't, you know, bleed out and die."

"What about this?" Mike pointed at a concave section of the slab blocking the tomb. It was a rounded indentation, about waist-high, and roughly the size of a man's belly.

"What are you suggesting?" Aruna frowned.

"Oh, come on," the captain sighed. "We all know what he's suggesting. And it's humiliating, so let's get it over with."

Captain Kevin lumbered up to the portal to push his paunch into the indentation. Strangely, his bloated stomach was a perfect fit.

An eerie glow emanated from the skin-to-stone contact, and the granite began to move.

"Wait!"

It was Dani, pulling the captain away from the tomb. The

instant that the connection was broken, the light faded and the stone stopped moving.

"What did you do that for?" Mike asked. "The bloated belly thing was working."

"I just, I think maybe we should think before we do this," Dani said.

"Who are you and what have you done with my sister?" Mike asked with smile. But Dani thought he was only half kidding. "Why are you so cautious all of a sudden? This is it. This is the climax at the end of the book where the heroes get the treasure and emerge triumphant!"

"I saw something," she said quietly. "Above the door. Mummies."

"Excuse me?"

"I've been looking at all the funny drawings on the tomb," Dani said. "And they look like mummies."

The engravings were disturbingly detailed, leaving little to the imagination: terrifying creatures wrapped in rotting bandages that rose from ancient tombs to strangle, impale, and generally inconvenience anyone who ventured inside their forbidden resting place.

"Makes sense," the captain said. "Tombs like these are where mummies are buried. But where'd they put the *daddies*?"

The whole world ignored him.

"And these drawings really seem to say that moving the headstone is a bad idea," Dani noted.

"What headstone?" Captain Kevin asked.

"The one you just tried to move."

"I don't have time for this," Aruna interjected, moving Dani roughly aside. "And I'm not leaving here without that treasure." She grabbed Captain Kevin and pushed his prodigious belly into the indentation. Instantly, the eerie glow returned and the stones ground against one another. The granite barrier shifted again, and then started moving on its own.

"I did it! It's opening!" the captain cried. "I am amazing!!!"

Everyone's hair rose with static electricity like it had in the jungle. They looked ridiculous, but no one was laughing this time.

Stale steam spilled out from behind the stone as a strange amber light pulsed from the chamber within. The glow grew brighter, throbbing in time with unearthly noises emanating from inside.

Dani's insides grew cold.

This was a bad idea.

The captain pointed accusingly at Aruna.

"She did it. She pushed me!"

The noises grew louder and faster.

"Do you hear that?" Dani asked. "Does anybody else hear that?"

"Maybe that's how you say 'howdy' in Amazonian?" the captain suggested weakly.

The stone seal came to a stop, and blindingly bright light radiated from the opening. The sound of rattling bones could be heard over the incessant moaning.

"Hey, kid," the captain whispered nervously to Dani. "What's ancient and ugly and smells like death?"

"I don't know. What?"

"I don't know, either, but it's coming out of that tomb. . . ."

Suddenly, the top of the glowing pit burst apart with unimaginable force—rock and debris raining down in every direction.

And a horrific figure rose slowly out of its grave.

CHAPTER 28
I WANT MY MUMMY

CAPTAIN KEVIN, with Aruna's help, had accidentally triggered the temple's curse, resurrecting the spirits of horrifying mummies that would guard their tomb for all eternity.

It had been that kind of day.

"Take the boy!" the captain yelled. "He never laughs at my jokes anyway."

The thing screamed back in uncontrollable fury.

And Captain Kevin ran.

The creatures erupted from their tomb, spreading across the room in a frenzy of screams and tattered bandages. They were covered from head to toe in the rotting remains of their Interment wrappings, but they behaved more like vengeful spirits, flying wraithlike across the death chamber. Their faces were shriveled and decayed like old fruit covered in moldy beef jerky. Some still had legs, but many didn't, their long, broken spines weaving like snakes behind them as they tore through the air.

For the first few seconds, Mike stood beside his sister, frozen in shock.

Spirits aren't real, he thought. *They're made-up. This can't be happening.*

One of the deathly figures swooped down toward the kids, its skeletal hands raised like talons.

Aruna yanked them out of harm's way at the last second. Mike's book bag fell to the ground. The creature's claws tore through the fabric, turning the bag and its remaining books into confetti, with the thing's hands gouging deep, dark scratches into the stone below.

This IS happening, Mike's brain gibbered. *It's an ancient temple full of mummies, who are furious that their tomb has been violated. You wanted adventure? Well, here you go.*

"We've gotta get out of here," Dani whispered, her voice tight with fear. "Where's the captain?"

They turned to see Captain Kevin halfway across the room, running for his life.

"I want my *mummy!*" he cried.

Mike grabbed Dani's hand and raced after the captain—a poor decision in any situation, but right now fear was clouding Mike's judgment. He bent down, darting between the heavy crypts and flinching every time the sound of whipping bandages passed overhead.

The mummies seemed propelled by mindless rage, lashing out as they hunted for whoever had disturbed their eternal resting place. Their skeletal faces stretched into painful expressions as they screamed.

The kids raced around the corner of a large stone coffin

and nearly crashed into Captain Kevin, who was cowering behind it for protection.

"Go away," he hissed. "This is my hiding place. You'll lead them right to us!"

His words proved prophetic as a mummy burst through the tomb, followed by a smell so noxious that it made their eyes water.

"See?" Captain Kevin coughed through his tears. "Ugh, they're worse than that hot sauce."

The captain darted left and Dani yanked her brother to the right as the tattered demon swooped down. It dove after the captain and his glowing, gurgling stomach.

They're after the jewel, Mike realized.

Ducking and darting and dodging like a terrible quarterback, Captain Kevin swerved around the stone coffins. He dove behind a crypt and was once again face-to-face with Mike and Dani.

"Stop following me," he whispered. "You're like bad luck magnets, attracting death and doom and death-doom."

"They're not after *us*," Mike hissed back. "They're after *you*! And the jewel!"

The mummies flowed around the crypt, closing in on their victims from every side.

Mike felt his heart drop. He knew it was over. They were cornered.

He watched Captain Kevin curl up into a ball and start chanting: "There's no place like home. There's no place like home."

Dani buried her face into her brother's chest, and Mike

tried desperately not to wet himself in his last few moments of life. He could feel the breath of the monsters as they moved in for the kill.

Then, suddenly, the creatures stopped.

Mike opened his eyes, but only a little.

He watched the mummies howl and fly across the room like banshees, away from Captain Kevin and the kids.

"What just happened?" Dani asked.

Mike carefully peered over the crypt and saw Aruna emerging from the tomb, glowing jewels clutched in her hands.

"They're after Aruna!" Mike exclaimed. "She took the jewels!"

The first of the mummified demons bore down on her. At the last second, Aruna dropped to one knee and raised her sword over her head. The mummy passed above her, instantly cleaved in two by her weapon. The two halves fell lifelessly to the ground, twin piles of rags and bones and dust.

Watching from behind their stone coffin, Dani cheered. "Yeah! Eat wall, ya dumb mummies!" Seeing that these things weren't as tough as they looked, she leapt up to join in.

"Dani! No!" Mike yelled.

But it was too late.

Another of the resurrected dead scrabbled toward Dani, baring its jagged teeth.

Using the moves that Aruna had shown her, Dani quickly sidestepped the spirit. She grabbed its bandages as it passed and used the creature's momentum to slam it into the nearest coffin.

The mummy shattered like pottery, shards tinkling to the floor at her feet.

Mike gaped at his sister. She was kicking serious mummy butt.

"*Welp*, it looks like you don't need me . . ." Captain Kevin said, skittering away.

Mike had no time for the captain's antics. Snatching one of the tall brass candleholders beside him, Mike spun it around his head, nearly hitting himself in the face. He quickly regained control, however, wielding the three-foot ornament like a weapon.

"Let's dance!" he yelled at the writhing creatures bombarding him.

Two mummies skittered across the room at him, swerving through the obstacle course of tombs.

Mike cocked the candlestick over his shoulder, dropping into a batter's stance. As the first mummy reached him, he swung for the fences. The crack of breaking bones filled the room as it shattered into thousands of pieces, before raining down like hailstones.

That one season of baseball was finally paying off.

The second bandaged banshee swooped in from the other side—and Mike swung in the other direction with everything he had. He wasn't officially a switch-hitter, but you wouldn't know it from the way the candlestick knocked the stuffing out of the attacking mummy. It flew straight into the nearest wall, where it broke apart like a two-thousand-year-old piñata filled with dust candy and dead bugs.

"Four down, two to go!" Dani cried.

"Uh-oh. I don't think so," Aruna warned. Still clutching her jewels in one hand and her sword in the other, she nodded toward the remains of the mummy she had destroyed, which seemed to be pulling itself back together. And it did not look happy.

"Oh, no," Mike said. He should've known this was too good to be true.

"Aruna," he shouted. "Drop the treasure!"

She didn't.

Aruna raised her sword at the mummies diving toward her from the ceiling. The revived creature—its head still split into two jagged shards—rose up behind Aruna and grabbed her wrist.

She cried out, dropping the weapon and her last jewel. The color drained from her arm, as tiny rivulets of black oil snaked out across her skin. Aruna's hand shriveled into a twisted claw and the entire limb decayed like a burning log.

"No!" Dani yelled, running to help her. But it was already too late.

Two other creatures fell upon Aruna, ensnaring her in a web of bandage and bone.

Moving at incredible speed, the three abominations pulled her across the floor, sweeping up the jewels with them. They flew back into the tomb, disappearing into the sickly bright light.

CHAPTER 29
AND MY MUMMY WANTS YOU

ARUNA WAS GONE.

"Nooooo!" Dani cried, her eyes brimming with tears. Blindly, she stumbled for the tomb, but Mike grabbed her, pulling her back.

"You can't," he said. Dani struggled against his grip, refusing to give in.

"We have to get out of here," he yelled, one hand on Dani, the other still holding his candlestick. The two of them were standing out in the open, a surefire way to get taken by the mummies that were still circling the room.

Dani kept pulling. Yes, maybe Aruna had betrayed them. And maybe Aruna hadn't been who she'd said she was. And maybe a lot of other things that Dani didn't want to think about right then. But to Dani, Aruna had also been kind and supportive, and she had even saved her from the caiman in the river. Dani couldn't just leave her.

Dani strained for the tomb just as a mummy swooped down toward Mike. It grabbed him under his arms and lifted him off the ground.

"Momo!" Dani yelled.

She cringed, bracing herself and expecting to see her brother succumb to the same decaying contagion that had infected Aruna.

But it didn't happen.

Hope surged inside her. Maybe it took skin-to-skin contact, she thought. The fabric of Mike's shirt was acting as a thin shield. For the moment, anyway . . .

"Don't let it touch your skin!" cried Dani.

The mummy flew Mike wildly around the room, craning its neck forward, its open mouth moving toward the flesh of Mike's exposed neck.

Dani held her breath.

Mike threw his arms up, ramming the heavy candlestick over his head and through the monster's empty eye socket, shattering its skull.

The thing recoiled, losing its grip. Mike fell and his body slammed hard against the corner of one of the crypts, bouncing off to collapse on the ground below.

The mummy with the newly shattered skull was flying blind. It crashed headlong into the snakelike face of one of the kneeling statues, exploding into bits.

Dani ran to her brother. He was hurt, badly. His leg lay twisted in a way that made her stomach queasy, and he was clutching his side like he'd broken a rib. Maybe two.

Dani didn't think. She just moved.

"Try not to scream," she whispered as she hooked her hands under his arms and pulled him across the floor. Mike's face contorted in pain, his hand slapping over his mouth.

As quickly and as gently as she could, Dani dragged him to a narrow space between one of the crypts and the wall. It wasn't much of a hiding space, but it was all they had; she hoped Captain Kevin had found a good one, too. Looking down at her brother's pained face, Dani knew that this was her fault.

If she had listened to him, they wouldn't have been standing out in the open, and he wouldn't have gotten hurt. If she had listened to him at the very beginning of this trip, or any of the other times he'd warned her on the river or in the jungle, they wouldn't be in this situation.

All along she had thought this was an adventure—and maybe it was. But it was not a game. It was not *pretend*.

People got hurt. Rube. Vincent. And now her brother. And Aruna? Aruna might be gone forever.

Dani hadn't realized it at the time, but in her desire to have fun and go "exploring" like Bermuda Betty, she had put them all in danger. She had been too reckless.

Since she was little, Dani had always thought that her brother was too much of a worrywart. And that because of the one time—ONE TIME—he hadn't watched her closely enough, he lived a life of caution and fear. She had been so young that she didn't even remember the incident. So while she took risks all the time, he seemed afraid to take any at all.

But now she wasn't so sure. When someone else is worried about you all the time, you don't have to worry about yourself. It frees you up to be bold. It was easy to be brave when she knew her brother was there. He'd been her bodyguard and safety net her entire life. And she loved him for it.

Now it was her turn to take care of him.

"No more adventuring," she finally said aloud. "I gotta get you home, Mike."

He looked up at her. It was the first time he could ever remember her calling him "Mike" instead of "Momo."

She stole a glance up at the mummies swooping and darting through the air like a swarm of zombie jellyfish.

"Why aren't they attacking?" Dani whispered.

"I don't know," Mike said quietly. "Maybe they can't really see us. You know, because they don't have any eyeballs. Maybe they only attack when they hear us."

"Hear us with what?" Dani turned back to him. "They don't have ears. Or brains for that matter. Or any working organs at all."

"I don't know! I'm just guessing!" said Mike.

Dani wasn't used to her brother not having the answer. And as she looked around, trying to figure out what to do next, knowing it was up to her, she suddenly felt scared.

She wondered, *Do adventurers get scared?*

Slowly rising to her feet, Dani peered over the edge of the crypt, looking for the safest way back to the stairs. She saw tattered strips of bandages on the ground—rotting leftovers from their battles with the creatures—and she suddenly got an idea.

"Wait here," Dani whispered. Before Mike could stop her, she dropped to her belly and army-crawled toward the bandages. A few seconds later she was back.

"Here," she said, handing Mike the filthy wrappings.

"No thank you," he said. "I'll pass."

"Too bad," Dani said firmly as she wrapped a strip of the rotting bandage around her arm. "If they can't touch our skin, they can't, you know, make us shrivel up and stuff."

"Oh," he said, realizing she had a point. "Good idea."

"Thanks." Dani beamed.

Mike grabbed the nearest strip of bandage and wrapped it around his neck.

Once they had covered themselves as thoroughly as they could, Dani peered over the crypt again.

"Okay, we're going to try to make it to the stairs. But first I have to find Captain Kevin."

"Forget him," snapped Mike. "He clearly forgot about us."

"No," Dani said firmly. "We have to find him. We're not losing anyone else today."

"Come on, Dani! Didn't we just go through this with Aruna?"

But Dani's mind was made up. She wasn't letting anyone else get hurt. She raced out of their hiding place, leaving her brother behind.

Her eyes searched the room and found Captain Kevin silently moving from crypt to crypt, drawing closer and closer to the central tomb and the jewels inside it. He peered into the white-hot light radiating from the opening.

Holding her breath, Dani raced over. She reached up behind the captain and yanked him away from the tomb.

The captain screamed through the noxious rags Dani had wrapped around one of her hands, kicking and flailing like he was on fire.

"Calm down," Dani whispered. "It's me."

"Don't sneak up on a guy like that," Captain Kevin hissed. "I thought you were one of those . . . things."

"Sorry," she replied. "I didn't think anything could scare you."

"Scared? *Pfff*. I wasn't scared. Startled. *Startled* is a better word. Never startle me, Dani. What if I'd karate-chopped your little head off? You gotta be more careful."

"And we gotta get out of here," Dani said adamantly. She peered up at the circling mummified phantoms. "Now."

"I'm not leaving without those jewels," he insisted.

"You go in there and you'll never come out," Dani warned.

"But they're right there! Come on! What happened to my little copilot?"

"She's watching your *aft*," Dani said. Her brow furrowed. "Please, Captain. I'm begging you. I don't want anything to happen to you."

The captain turned to her. A stern look on his face said he was not going to be swayed by the pleas of a little girl, but then he paused, staring at Dani's flushed cheeks and wet eyes. Her tiny hands pulling on his arm were shaking. She was scared, but not for herself. She was genuinely worried for him.

"If you go in there," she sniffed, "you're never gonna come out. Just like . . . like . . ."

For once in his life, Captain Kevin seemed to let down his guard.

"I feel bad about her, too, kid," said the captain. "Honestly, but . . ." He looked from Dani to the tomb entrance and then back to Dani, and she could have sworn she saw something shift inside him.

"I can't believe I'm saying this," he sighed. "But I guess the jewel lodged in my intestines will have to do. Let's go."

Dani didn't need to be told twice. She and the captain bolted across the room like jackrabbits; Dani headed toward Mike, while the captain headed for the exit atop the stairs. The mummies, circling high above their tomb, turned at the sudden movement.

"We have to get Momo!" Dani yelled.

"Who? Oh, right! Sure. Yeah. Of course," said the captain. "Forgot. Sorry."

Covering his head, Captain Kevin joined Dani and headed toward Mike. They found him somehow on his feet, ready for them. Mike threw an arm over each of their shoulders and they quickly hobbled for the stairs.

The mummies snarled in fury. They swooped down to ground level, one after another, whipping between the granite-encased coffins after their prey.

Stumbling up the stairs, Dani hoped against hope that they'd make it to the top in time. Suddenly, she heard the sound of massive stones grinding against each other—again.

Something had been triggered.

"Another booby trap?" asked Captain Kevin.

Without warning, the stairs moved. The sections of the staircase that had been horizontal—the part the captain, Mike, and Dani were standing on—suddenly shifted, slanting downward. What had been a flight of stairs quickly became NOT a flight of stairs. It became a ridiculously steep stone slide.

Screaming in unison, the three slid down the ramp, rapidly gaining speed toward the writhing creatures below.

FROM THE JOURNAL OF CAPTAIN
KEVIN ADVENTURESON

Always look out for number one.

That's my motto.

Well, it's one of my mottoes. The others include "Look both ways before you cross the street" and "Don't eat yellow snow."

Oh, and "The customer is always right," since I'm usually the customer.

I guess I have a lot of mottoes.

But my number one motto is "Look out for number one."

In most situations, I find that I'm the most important person I know, so I have to put my own safety and security first.

I mean, if I don't protect myself, who's going to be left to protect everybody else, huh?

So, don't be fooled by those people who say, "Do unto others," and "Obey the golden rule." They're just trying to sell you a bumper sticker.

In conclusion, always look out for number one.

Especially in the snow.

Unless you're on a horse ranch.
Then look out for number two.

CHAPTER 30
SAND IN MY SHORTS

DANI, MIKE, AND THE CAPTAIN careened down the makeshift slide. The mummies leapt into the air at their incoming prey, hungry mouths open and razor-sharp talons spread wide.

Mike was genuinely terrified and sure they were gonna die. Again.

Then the floor opened up.

The three of them slid right under the mummies and through the opening, tumbling down into darkness.

Mike hit the floor of the lower level with a force that knocked the air from his lungs. The panel above them slammed shut, sealing them in total blackness.

"Are you guys okay?" Mike heard Dani call out.

"No," he groaned. "I'd find it very difficult to describe my condition right now as 'okay.' If my leg wasn't broken before, I think that fall did the trick."

"Oh, no, I'm sorry, Momo," Dani said sympathetically. "Captain Kevin?"

"Yeah, right here," he called. "I'm okay. I landed on something fairly soft that broke my fall."

"That would be me," Mike said through gritted teeth.

"Oh, sorry about that." The captain quickly climbed off Mike.

"Why haven't those things come after us?" Dani asked.

"I don't know," Mike said, trying to peer up through the gloom to the floor above them. "Maybe they can't go too far from their tomb. Or maybe there's a magical Bermuda Triangle unicorn-enchantment spell that binds that chamber in a mystical energy vortex of wonder."

The pain was making him snarky.

"Where are we?" Dani asked. "The ground feels, I don't know, gritty. Sandy."

"Oh. Maybe this will help," Captain Kevin said. He flicked a lighter he had pulled from one of his many pockets and tore off a length of Mike's mummy wrap.

The fabric caught fire, and soon a weak glow filled the room.

"It's a pit," Mike said.

"Well, it *could* benefit from a little interior decorating," the captain agreed.

The room, if you could call it that, was basically an empty chamber carved into the earth. There were no windows or doors. Other than the sealed trapdoor above their heads and a few odd-looking water spouts that stuck out of the walls near the ceiling, there wasn't much to it.

"What do you suppose those are for?" Dani asked, pointing at the spigots above them.

And that's when it happened.

From each of the four tubes protruding from the walls, sand gushed into the room, spilling onto the floor.

"Yes!" the captain cried, quickly situating himself under one of the flows, and opening his mouth wide. Seconds later, he was gagging and spitting.

"*Augh*. Gah. It's sand!" he coughed. "I thought it was cornmeal."

"Why would you possibly think it was cornmeal?" Mike asked.

"Well, maybe we don't all see the glass as half empty, Mr. Negativity," the captain spat back, actually spitting out bits of sand as he did.

"So, you honestly thought that the people who built this temple might have decided, 'Hey, for this next room, instead of scaring them to death, let's serve them lunch!'"

"Well, our luck has to turn around at some point, right?" the captain said. "It can't get worse and worse and worse. That's not fair!"

Mike didn't know what to say to that. He was not about to have the "life's not always fair" talk with a man who was old enough to be his father.

"Guys, I think we have a problem," Dani said, looking down. The sand was already up to her ankles. "If this sand keeps coming . . ."

She didn't have to finish the sentence. They all knew what would happen.

Mike tried to control his rapid breathing and frantically thought back to every book he'd read where the heroes survived quicksand or being trapped in a gigantic hourglass. Unfortunately, he couldn't come up with anything that would help them here. All he could think about was how every novel's main character always stepped up to become a better person by the end, turning into the hero he or she needed to be. He had hoped that Captain Kevin might follow that path. But would he?

"Oh, God, we'll be buried *aliiiiiive!*" the captain screamed.

"No. Now, stop it," Dani said. "Every room we've been in has a trapdoor, or secret panel, or hidden something. We just have to find it."

Dani beat on the walls. Mike wasn't ready to try standing yet, but he pawed at the base of the wall, looking for a passage.

The captain, however, was not up to the task. He dropped down onto his backside, defeated, letting the stream from above pour over his head.

"I never knew my parents, you know," Captain Kevin sighed, bravado draining from his face and voice. "I was an orphan. But I was scrappy. I fended for myself, stealing, tricking tourists. It's what you do to survive."

"I'm sorry," Mike said. "But now is not the time to tell us your life story. We need your help." The sand was in his shoes now, and in his shorts. It was everywhere.

"I was basically alone until, oh, I must've been nine or ten. I didn't really keep track of the years," the captain continued. He hadn't heard a word Mike had said. "Until I met . . . Dagger."

He smiled at the thought.

"I hung around him every chance I had. He took pity on me and didn't shoo me away like the others. And he was strong and brave—and a man of the world, always decked out in a panama hat and one of those long duster coats. He was everything I wanted to be. He was a Shipwrecker."

The sand was up to the captain's shoulders now and rising like the evening tide.

"You can crawl to the top of the sand, you know," Dani informed him.

"Plus, you're still sitting down," Mike added with more than a hint of frustration. "If you stand up, it's only up to your waist."

"A diamond mine in the Congo. That was his downfall." The captain was lost in the memory. "I never saw him again. I lost my hero and now you're about to lose yours. Me, buried under the sand. Never to be seen again. You must be devastated!"

Mike had heard enough. Even at death's door, this idiotic idiot was an idiot.

"You're no *hero*. You're a fraud and a coward," barked Mike. "Every time, every *single* time, you run away when things get tough."

"Not true," the captain protested. "Name one time."

"When the caimans climbed on your boat, you ran. When the freighter started moving, you were out of there. When the mummies came out of the tomb, you bolted. Literally, the *very first time* we saw you, you were running away from an angry mob. You *always* run away. Well, look around, 'Captain'; this is one situation you *can't* run away from."

"You're right," Captain Kevin sobbed, his voice catching in his throat. "He's right. The boy has found my one fatal flaw."

"One?" Mike balked. "One?! That's just scratching the surface of your barnacle-covered hull. You're useless. Insensitive. Selfish. Greedy. Immature. A liar. Cowardly. Self-aggrandizing. Stupid. And, with God as my witness, you smell like a dead hippo that's been rotting in the sun!"

"I do!" confessed the captain, who was crying actual tears now. "I do smell. I always have. It must be so unpleasant for those around me. I should probably see a doctor."

"Stop it!" said Mike. "It ruins it if you agree with me!"

Captain Kevin was just wailing now, making strange, elongated vowel sounds like a heartsick sea cow.

Mike realized that the captain had found a way to run, even in a locked room; it was just a mental escape this time instead of a physical one. Mike cursed himself for ever thinking that he could count on Captain Kevin for anything. If they were going to survive, it was up to the Gonzalez kids. Maybe it always had been up to them.

He turned to see if Dani had made any progress.

But his sister was gone.

CHAPTER 31
SAND DIVING

"**D**ANI!" MIKE SCREAMED.

She was gone. What had happened to her? Was she buried under the sand? Had one of those mummified monsters found a way in and taken her?

He cursed. He'd been so distracted by the captain that he'd let something horrible happen to his sister.

"Dani!" he yelled again.

And then something under the sand grabbed his leg.

He screamed, visions of being dragged under by some hideous sandworm filling his brain. But before he could react, the thing beneath him pulled its way up his leg and Dani's head popped out of the sand.

Mike immediately wrapped his arms around his sister, hugging her. She was gasping for breath, but otherwise appeared unharmed.

"What happened?" he asked frantically. "Are you okay? What were you doing?"

"We never checked the bottom," she said between deep breaths. "The floor."

"So you went down there without telling me? You could have suffocated, you dork!" He hugged her again.

"But I didn't, you dummy," she argued. "I knew there had to be a way to empty out all this sand, you know, for the *next* time they want to kill people. So, unless they have the world's biggest vacuum cleaner or something, there has to be some kind of drain, right?"

What she was saying made sense, and Mike was upset that he hadn't thought of it. But he was more upset that his sister had done something so dangerous and impulsive—even though *dangerous* and *impulsive* were practically tattooed on her forehead.

"You can't do things like that," he scolded. "Why would you do that?"

"Because I got us into this situation, Momo. I wanted to go on this adventure. I got you hurt by those mummies. It's my fault and I need to fix it."

"It's not your fault," Mike started, but Dani wasn't done talking.

"I couldn't see anything down there, obviously, but I felt something like a ring. Like a brass ring, that flipped up from the floor. I thought maybe if we could turn it . . ." she started. "But it was hard to turn and I was running out of air. That's when I came up."

"I'm going down!" the captain shouted, and he dove face-first into the sand like a high diver into an Olympic pool. He hit the sand with a hard *SMACK*, his mouth and nose digging a few inches in before coming to an abrupt stop. He groaned. "Man overboard."

Mike ignored him and turned back to his sister.

"You can't go down there. Too risky," Mike said. "*Unless* we have a plan." He pointed at the tubes that were still spilling sand into their prison.

"Do you think one of those tubes would fit through the ring?"

Dani looked.

"I think so."

"If we can get one loose, we might be able to use it to turn the ring," Mike theorized. "It'll give us more leverage."

"Cool," she said. "Boost me up."

Within minutes, Dani had twisted one pipe free and pulled it from the hole. It was a good three feet long.

"It's longer than I thought," Mike observed. "If we can get the other three out, we might be able to solve the other part of our problem. Breathing."

"I'm on it," the captain said, hurrying across the indoor sand dune and immediately shoving his head into the sand like a frightened ostrich.

One minute and eight inches of sand later, Dani had retrieved the rest of the tubes and Mike had attached three of them together into a single nine-foot-long pipe.

"Hopefully, this can work kind of like a snorkel," he explained. "Providing air for whoever is under the sand trying to twist that ring."

"I'll go," Dani said, picking up the pipe. "You can't do it with your leg. And Captain Kevin doesn't seem to understand that this isn't water."

She looked over to where the captain was doing the

backstroke across the sea of sand like a mermaid in the desert.

"I'll have all the air I need with the pipe you put together," she said.

"Hold on. Hold on," Mike insisted. "I don't even know if it will work." He wanted to run the whole thing through in his head one more time to be sure.

"There's no more time to think about it, Momo. We have to act. Now."

She was right, and he knew it.

"Okay, yes. Go. I trust you," Mike said. "I know you can do it."

Dani gave him a quick hug, strapped the short length of pipe to her belt, and burrowed into the sand.

His hands sweating, Mike pushed the long pipe after her, watching it descend inch after inch. He realized that, although he was scared for her, he was thinking about his sister in a new way. She was brave. Fiery. Full of ideas. He had seen his worst fears realized when she'd disappeared, but she had survived on her own. She could handle this—he believed that—and he had to let her try.

Suddenly, through the far end of the tube, he heard her take a long gulp of air, and his heart started beating again.

She was okay.

For now.

It seemed like hours passed, but it couldn't have been more than a few minutes or the sand would have already buried them all. As it was, Mike could easily touch the ceiling, even from his kneeling position. Time was almost up.

"She'll be okay," the captain said, attempting compassion. "But even if she isn't, you won't be around much longer to feel bad about it!" Captain Kevin made a prolonged choking noise and fell over, playing dead.

* * *

Deep beneath layer upon layer of sand, Dani crawled blindly, like a mole in a tunnel, trying to keep her sense of direction. She could still feel which way was down; she just hoped she wasn't veering too far to the right or left. She couldn't afford to spend much time searching for that ring.

It was harder than she thought and deeper than she remembered, and the effort to keep digging was exhausting. She hadn't wanted to worry Momo, but she was scared. It was pitch dark and the sand was pushing in on her from every side, making her feel claustrophobic and trapped.

Finally, thankfully, her fingers brushed the floor of the pit. She had made it to the bottom. Now she scoured the ground for the indentation where the ring lay.

It wasn't there.

Had she gone too far in one direction? Maybe, but which way? She didn't have time to search the entire floor. Which direction should she go? She had to choose.

* * *

At the top of the room, Mike pushed the long tube down another few inches. Now there were only three or four inches of the tube protruding above the surface of the sand. This was as far down as he could safely push it.

"Nice kitty," the captain babbled.

"Quiet!" Mike whispered. "I think I heard something."

Mike put his ear to the end of the tube, straining to listen. "I found it."

It was Dani, using her air tube as a makeshift telephone.

"Hold on," she said. He heard her take a deep breath and then silence.

CHAPTER 32
WAIT, YOU MEAN THEY DIDN'T ALL DIE?

IT FELT LIKE THE FLOOR had dropped out from under them.

The mound in the center of the room fell away, with the sand on the edges spiraling into the void like a whirlpool. Mike and the captain swirled down into the sandstorm below.

They slammed into a metal grate, the roar of sand still flooding past them.

As the pounding finally relented, Mike lifted his head and saw his sister grinning at him.

Dani had done it.

She'd found a release gate and opened it, clearing the room of sand. It had filtered through a heavy grate that kept them from getting washed away, too. And from the bones scattered around them, it had clearly sifted out the remains of those who had not been so lucky.

"So . . . worth the risk?" she asked.

"Worth the risk," Mike agreed sheepishly. "Thanks, Dani."

"Yes, nice work, kid," the captain said, ruffling Dani's hair. "That was a test and you aced it. I would've done it myself, but I needed to see how you reacted under pressure."

Now that the immediate danger had passed, Mike saw that Captain Kevin's sanity seemed to have returned. And so had his penchant for lying.

"Sooooo . . . I made up all that phony-baloney stuff about my childhood so that you'd believe it was up to you to save us. And it worked! Good job."

"Uh, thanks, Captain Kevin," Dani said politely.

"Guys, look!"

Mike was pointing to the far end of the grate, where a doorway stood open. There was no giant stone tablet blocking it, no wall hiding it. It was just open.

Dani and Captain Kevin helped Mike to his feet, and then the three stepped through the doorway into a small alcove featuring a spiral staircase. And unlike every other set of stairs they had encountered in the vast crypt, this one, thankfully, was going up.

"I don't think they ever expected anyone to survive to see this level," Mike said, gesturing back at the bones on the grate. "This may actually be a way out . . . you know, or another death trap."

"Never look a gift exit in the mouth," Captain Kevin said, pushing past them to head up the twisting stairs. Dani quickly followed, and Mike hobbled after them.

The stairs finally ended at a stone doorway that opened easily when Dani pressed against it. They found themselves back inside one of the main chambers of the temple.

"We're right back where we started," moaned the captain, always a ray of sunshine on a cloudy day.

"No, we're higher," Mike said. "We're above most of it. We have to be."

"So, now what?" Dani asked as she peered around the dark interior. "Which way do we go?"

"There!" Mike's eyes lit up as he pointed. "My trail."

Still lying on the ground a few feet away was one of the pages he had torn from one of his books.

"Guess those useless books came in handy after all," Captain Kevin conceded.

Mike picked up each page as they followed the trail back to the temple entrance. All his life, his books had provided him with an escape . . . and now this torn-up book was *literally* helping him escape. Much as Mike had wanted to, he knew he couldn't put his book back together, but he felt like, at the very least, he owed it the honor of a decent burial.

And, of course, he'd buy a new copy of the sacrificed book as soon as he got home.

The reptile head where they had entered was still a pile of rubble, but there were other exits nearby. Apparently, the designers of the temple were much more interested in keeping people out than keeping them in.

Before they knew it, they had stepped outside for the first time in what felt like days. Mike had never been so happy to see the clear blue sky and breathe fresh tropical air.

"We did it, Momo." Dani grinned. "We took a risk, we had a real adventure, and we survived!"

"Yeah, we did!" Mike jumped into the air, running like a little kid. "Ow, my leg."

He hugged the trees. He kissed the ground. He high-fived a plant.

"Hello, tree! Hello, sky! Hello, banana!" he grinned, limping over to a banana tree and grabbing a handful from a low-hanging bunch.

"Come on, Captain!" Dani called. "Banana time!"

There was no response.

Mike turned to look.

Captain Kevin was gone.

"*Mmmfshhfr!*" Mike cursed through a mouthful of banana. "He did *not* just leave us here."

"He wouldn't do that," Dani said. "Look!"

She was pointing at the small opening where they had first entered the temple.

There was light flickering inside the darkness. Light from someone's torch.

And then the captain stuck his face out of the hole.

"Oh, hey, guys," he said awkwardly. "I was, uh, I forgot something in there."

He stood up, brushing the dirt off his hands and looking everywhere but at their eyes.

"What did you do?" Mike asked suspiciously.

"Nothing. Less than nothing. The inverse of nothing."

"That means you did something," said Dani.

Mike felt his legs wobbling beneath him, though he wasn't sure if it was from anger, or fatigue, or his injury—or all three.

"Hey, is the ground shaking?" Dani asked.

The pebbles on the ground were bouncing like tiny droplets of grease in a hot pan.

"What did you do?" Mike demanded again, grabbing Captain Kevin by the collar.

"Well, they were just sitting there," the captain explained. "I mean, it's not fair that I had to leave completely empty-handed."

The ground lurched once more and Dani grabbed Mike to keep him from falling over.

"So, I took two jewels. Big whoop!" the captain said. "From the eyes of the snake-reptile thing where we entered."

"Those aren't yours," Dani said. "You shouldn't have done that."

The captain waved her off.

"Please. Who's going to miss two little jewels?"

As if in answer to his question, the ground lifted beneath their feet.

The temple was moving.

It wouldn't have surprised Mike if Captain Kevin's last-minute greedy maneuver was about to bring down the entire structure, or the entire valley for that matter.

But the ancient building wasn't collapsing.

It was rising.

Out of the earth.

Just like the fifth drawing in the temple that Dani had seen.

"Run," Dani said. "Run!"

Grabbing Mike under the arms, Dani and the captain scrambled away from the temple, even as the dirt beneath their feet roiled like the crest of a tidal wave.

Larger and larger sections of the pyramid-like structure rose up out of the ground. Cracks in the dirt shot out like lightning bolts, radiating in all directions from the temple as the earth crumbled and shattered.

The rumbling was louder than anything Mike had ever heard, like the sound of a hundred locomotives passing right under his feet. He could feel the vibrations rattling his teeth, his bones, his skull.

Then, impossibly, a raw, terrible roar echoed across the rain forest, overpowering the noise of the splitting earth.

Mike looked back at the gigantic temple rising up behind them.

It was screaming.

It was alive.

CHAPTER 33
OH, CRAP!

CAPTAIN KEVIN SCREAMED like a howler monkey.

The thing behind them was beyond massive. It was like a towering office building getting up to stretch its legs, or an entire hillside deciding to go out for a morning jog.

"This can't be happening," Mike said.

"You can keep saying that," the captain hollered. "But it's not listening."

The gargantuan structure was no longer underground. It rose high above the tallest tree, its base as wide as a city block. The thousands and thousands of huge stones that made up its walls and floors and chambers were shifting, moving, sliding, and grinding against one another.

It was changing.

"This is your fault!" Dani yelled at the captain for the first time. "You had to go back and steal something that wasn't yours! That wasn't right and now you're in big trouble."

"How was I to know the entire stinkin' place would come to life like . . . like . . . ?"

"Like a mummy's curse!" Mike yelled back. "You've never heard of the mummy's curse? You steal the jewels, you trigger the curse!"

"Okay, Mr. 'I don't believe in Bigfoot.' Someone sure is changing their tune now," the captain taunted.

Mike felt like his mind was melting as, behind them, the thing that had once been a temple slowly shifted into something else entirely—a creature made of rock and rage, glowing with the power of the stones in its belly, just like the glistening barnacles on the shipwrecked ships and the two stolen gems in the captain's pocket.

"That has to be a building code violation," Captain Kevin yelled.

The thing took one monumental step forward, and the earth shook so violently that Mike, Dani, and the captain were nearly thrown to the ground.

"It has legs!" Captain Kevin cried. "The temple's got legs!"

The stone behemoth took its second step, crossing the clearing toward them in gargantuan strides. Dirt and debris rained down like flakes of dandruff the size of baseballs.

Once again, they ran for their lives, Captain Kevin and Dani helping Mike hobble along as quickly as possible.

With the mummies, Mike had been scared. Now he was terrified. This was like being chased by an earthquake on legs.

"It's too big," Dani cried. "We can't outrun it!"

"I'm going as fast as I can," Mike shouted.

"Pick him up!" Dani yelled at the captain.

"What?" Captain Kevin spat back. "How does that help me?"

"Just do it!" Dani demanded.

The captain stooped, and with great effort, hoisted the boy over his shoulder. Puffing, he ran to catch up with Dani.

The ground shook beneath them as the structure took another step.

"This isn't helping," Captain Kevin wheezed. "The only difference is that now he's even *more* of a pain in my neck. We're not gonna make it."

"The plane!" Mike yelled back.

Several hundred yards ahead of them sat the biplane that Rube and Vincent had used to track them to the temple.

"Yes. Good. I was about to suggest that," Captain Kevin lied.

But the small plane was a dot in the distance and the temple monster was quickly gaining ground. They hobbled over a fallen log, and seconds later, the giant's next step crushed the log to kindling.

Mike's stomach clenched as he realized they would never make it to the plane alive. The temple creature was too big and too fast. He had to come up with a plan and come up with it right now. He thought back to their strategy at the shipwreck graveyard.

"Dani! Run to the left! Now!"

Dani did as she was told, making a hard left into the thicker vegetation.

"Captain, the other way!" Mike yelled, still hanging over the man's shoulder. The captain ran to the right.

The leviathan's foot slammed down right where they had been standing.

As they ran, Mike plunged his hand into Captain Kevin's pocket.

"*Heeey!*" the captain yelled in protest. "What did I do, officer? I know my rights!"

Mike pulled out the stolen jewels and held them high in the air. He wasn't about to die for a few rocks.

"Is this what you want?" he bellowed up at the living rock.

Slowly, like a mountaintop shifting on its base, the thing turned toward them.

"Come on. Come and get 'em!"

"Hey! Those aren't yours!" the captain cried in protest.

"Well, they're not yours, either," Mike yelled back.

Captain Kevin grappled with Mike, struggling to wrest the jewels from his hand.

"I stole those fair and square!" the captain insisted. "They're mine!"

"Not anymore!" Mike cocked his arm back and threw the jewels as hard as he could toward the thing that had once been the stationary temple.

What happened next was something Mike could never adequately explain to anyone else. Mike knew that in the years to come, every time that he would try to talk about what happened, it would sound far too ridiculous and he would stop; it was just too stupid.

The temple sat on the jewels.

The entire pyramid had come to life, pulled itself out of the ground, transformed into a half building/half rock-monster, and then squatted down like a giant toddler over a toilet and sat on its missing jewels.

It was preposterous, and impossible—and utterly stupid.

Once again, the earth's crust rocked with the impact.

The mountainous living temple hesitated for a moment, resting on its laurels. A beat later, when it rose back up off the ground, the jewels were gone. Mike could only assume, as ridiculous as it sounded, that the thing had absorbed its treasure back into itself.

Through its stone butt.

The towering thing slowly turned away from them to face the vast pit where it had climbed out of the ground.

"Is it over?" Mike wondered aloud, not daring to hope. "Is it going back?"

"Well, it got what it came for," the captain sighed. "Technically, it got what *I* came for, thanks to you. But yes, I'd imagine it's done. It can go back to being an underground death trap again."

Captain Kevin gently set Mike back on the ground as they stared up at the backside of the mammoth figure, waiting to see if it would take its first step toward the hole.

It didn't.

It started to squat.

"Wait, wait, wait, wait, wait," said a panicked Mike. "What is it doing?"

"*Uuuuugh!*" Captain Kevin groaned, clutching his stomach. His belly was glowing between his fingers. "I think we might have something else that belongs to him."

As the shadow of the descending figure fell over them,

Mike remembered the jewel that the captain had swallowed.

The temple wanted it back.

And now it was trying to sit on *them*.

"Looks like this is the end," Captain Kevin quipped, pointing up at the incoming rock buttocks. "Literally."

"Move! Move! Move!" Mike leapt onto the captain's back and kicked at him with his good leg like a jockey prodding his horse to run faster. They ran with no plan, no idea what to do, and no clue how they could possibly get away.

Then Mike heard it.

The whine of an engine—the sound of a biplane.

CHAPTER 34
STILL NOT THE END

DANI WAS DRIVING THE PLANE.

The captain carried Mike, racing to the clearing, and found Rube and Vincent's tiny biplane taxiing toward them. Well, Mike acknowledged, *taxiing* might be too generous a term.

The aircraft was weaving left and right, and then, to his surprise, it made a complete circle before righting itself and heading back in the right direction.

"What is she doing?" the captain asked.

"I don't think she can see out of the cockpit," Mike guessed.

Mike was right. Dani had clearly managed to get the plane started and moving, but she had the visibility of a gerbil in a Coke can.

Behind them, the stone Goliath rose to its feet, turning toward Captain Kevin and the jewel bouncing around in his belly.

"Come on," the captain said, helping Mike down off his

shoulder so he could hobble toward the oncoming plane. "We're almost there."

"There won't be enough time," Mike said, wincing with each step. "If she stops to let us on, that thing will crush us."

"Who said anything about stopping?" the captain laughed.

Suddenly, they saw Dani standing up on the seat. With the extra height, she saw that she was about to mow down her brother and the captain.

"Oh, no!" she cried.

"Jump!" the captain yelled.

Mike and Captain Kevin were now on either side of the plane's fuselage; they leapt into the air and each grabbed ahold of one of the wings.

"Ow!" Mike groaned.

The plane shuddered with the impact, but it held together.

"What the—" Dani said in shock.

"Keep going!" Mike yelled back. "Keep going!"

"THIS is your plan?" Dani balked.

"We're kind of winging it," Mike said.

"Was that a joke?" gasped the captain. "Did you just make a joke?"

"I'm a little delirious from the pain," said Mike. "Now go!"

Dani saw they were heading straight for the bellowing temple monster. She pushed the little plane as fast as it could go, darting between the creature's legs a split second before it fell back, trying to sit on them.

"Why does that temple keep sitting on his bottom?" she asked.

"He's a *house sitter*," the captain said as he climbed from the wing up toward the cockpit. Reaching over across the other side of the plane, he helped Mike up and eased him into the front seat, where Dani quickly joined him.

But across the clearing, the squatting pyramid was rising up again.

Captain Kevin threw himself into the pilot's seat and turned the plane back toward the stone monster.

"What are you doing?" Mike said. "We want to get AWAY from that thing!"

"Not enough runway," Captain Kevin said. "Our only chance of taking off is going back across the clearing the way we just came."

"Great," Mike grumbled to himself. "Wouldn't it be easier to throw you and the jewel overboard?"

"What was that?" the captain called out. "Couldn't hear you over the engine!"

"I said, 'Good luck!'"

"Thanks!"

Captain Kevin accelerated as fast as he could, driving the plane across the bumpy clearing straight toward the monster.

The stone creature transformed again; long, thick clumps of stone broke away from its sides to form armlike structures.

"Oh, great," the captain said. "Now the thing has *armed* itself!"

The captain jerked the plane to the side just as the monster's fist-like appendage came down.

It smashed a hole in the jungle floor large enough to trap an elephant.

The captain muscled the plane back on course, its wing grazing the foot of the giant as they passed.

"So long, tall, dark, and stony." The captain waved.

Mike looked ahead and saw that the clearing ended in dense jungle in a few hundred feet.

"We're not out of the woods yet," Mike yelled.

"Hey, is that another joke?" the captain said. "Dani, your brother's working his funny bone!"

"I'm not joking," Mike yelled. "Pull up. Pull up!"

"We're not going fast enough," the captain explained.

"We're not going fast enough!" Dani echoed the captain, looking back over her shoulder at the temple monster.

It was no longer walking.

It was running.

BOOM!

The plane shook as the thing's foot hit the ground.

BOOM!

It was only two steps behind them—and the plane was twenty feet from a very unyielding thatch of trees.

BOOM!

Captain Kevin pulled back on the stick—hard—and the plane rose off the ground, heading straight for the trees.

Mike closed his eyes.

The wheels of the biplane ripped the leaves from the tops of the tallest branches as it clipped the roof of the jungle.

BOOM!

The giant's foot slammed down at the end of the clearing, cracking, snapping, and splintering dozens of trees under its mighty frame.

Mike held Dani tightly. They weren't going to make it.

The creature's massive stone hands reached out for the plane and clapped together like thunder.

FROM THE JOURNAL OF CAPTAIN
KEVIN ADVENTURESON

If you're reading this, that means I'm dead.

It's okay, you can weep for me. I'm worth it.

Dig deep. Ugly cry it all out.

I'll wait.

Right. Now that I'm dead, I think it's important to remember that everyone makes mistakes . . . except for me. In my case, I always did my best, better than anyone has ever done in human history. Also, I was very handsome. More handsome even than you've heard.

Yup. *That* handsome.

No matter what anyone tells you, I never took their share of the profits. I was just holding it for safekeeping. Actually, no matter what they tell you, I was only thinking of what was best for them. Unless they say I'm awesome, in which case, feel free to take their word for it.

In closing, I know I made the world a better place, and touched the lives of those closest to me in immeasurable ways. But rest assured, when I leave

this adventure for the next, know that there is only
one person who will miss me the most.
   Me.

CHAPTER 35
WHAT HAS SIX LEGS AND FLIES?

"**Y**OU SAVED US!"

Mike was stunned even more than he was relieved.

The temple monster's stone hands had missed them by inches, the resulting gust of wind nearly knocking them out of the sky. But to Mike's shock, the captain had managed to pull them out of the dive and away from the creature.

"Thank you, Captain Kevin!" Dani squealed, leaning out of her seat to give him a hug around the neck.

The captain blushed despite himself.

"The important thing is that everyone's safe," stated Captain Kevin. "Including me."

The captain coughed into his hand.

"And, even more importantly, I've still got the gem."

He coughed again, hard, and caught something in his hand.

It was the dislodged jewel from his stomach.

"I won't be rich, but it'll get me a down payment on a new boat."

"Wait," Mike said, his tone instantly growing cold. "Do you mean to tell me that you could have done that at any time? That you could have coughed that up whenever you wanted?"

"Hey, I'm a man of many talents." Captain Kevin smiled. "I have skills you kids can't imagine."

"That's not a skill," Mike barked. "It's disgusting. And the fact that you kept it in your stomach this whole time means you purposely *chose* to put all of us in danger instead of making things right."

"Well, I don't *choose* to look at it that way," the captain said awkwardly.

"Those cursed mummies were trying to get that jewel back! And what about the freighter? That gigantic freighter in the shipwreck graveyard was drawn toward you, too," Mike growled. "A fifty-ton stone monster came after us because of you and that stupid rock in your stomach!

"It was after YOU, not us! It wanted to sit on YOU!"

Mike's anger flared up like a raging fire. "All you needed to do was cough up that stupid stone so we wouldn't be crushed to death by a freaking walking building!"

"Well, we could spend all day trying to determine who endangered who and whose selfish actions put who at risk," the captain said. "But it's all water under the boat now."

Captain Kevin tipped the plane's right wing down and made a wide arc over the rain forest.

"Uhhh, why are we turning?" Dani asked.

"It's a shortcut. Back to the river," the captain said unconvincingly.

"But you're heading back over the temple area," she said.

"No, I'm not."

Mike sat up, instantly scouring the landscape below them.

"Yes, you are," he said. "There's the crater it crawled out of. What are you doing? That thing could be waiting for us!"

"I'm just doing a quick flyby to make sure we didn't leave any jewels lying in the crater. You know how when you get up from a nap on the couch, you sometimes leave some change behind on the pillows?" The captain sounded like he was trying to convince himself as much as the others. "Well, maybe this temple guy did the same thing. Dragged himself out of this two-thousand-year-old hole in the ground and accidentally dropped a fortune in priceless gems without noticing it."

"They're not yours!" Dani yelled.

"You're going to get us killed!" Mike screamed.

The captain didn't have time to respond as a living wall rose up in front of them, blocking out the sun.

The temple monster.

"Whoops," Captain Kevin said. "Where'd he come from? Hang on!"

The captain sent the plane spiraling off to the right, careening wildly past the creature, but it was now quickly losing altitude as it began to nosedive.

"Whoops," Captain Kevin said again.

"Stop saying *whoops*!" Mike hollered, his fingers gripping the edge of the plane like a vise.

The captain pulled back on the yoke with all the strength he had, muscling the biplane out of the dangerous dive seconds before it would have hit the ground.

"We're too low!" Dani cried as they flew mere inches above the foliage, giving the taller trees instant haircuts.

"Or not low enough," Captain Kevin retorted, dropping the plane even lower. They dipped down into the hole that had once housed the temple, and the captain craned his neck to look for any sparkling treasures.

"You really don't care about anyone or anything but yourself, do you?" Mike seethed as the plane circled the pit and finally climbed back up out of the hole. "You'd risk your own grandmother's life if you thought you could profit from it."

"Aw, quit your bellyachin'. I'm sure my grandmother's already dead," the captain said. "Besides, we're fine."

WHAM!

The plane rocked wildly as the stone creature took one last swipe; this time the tip of its massive hand connected with the tail of the plane.

The back of the fuselage shattered, pieces of fiberglass raining down like artificial snow onto the jungle floor.

The plane lurched uncontrollably. Then, reeling from the impact, it rolled.

Dani, who was not belted in beside her brother, slipped from the seat as the aircraft turned upside down.

Desperately, Mike reached out.

He caught her sleeve.

But it ripped.

Mike's heart ripped out with it.

Dani slipped away just as the plane righted itself. But instead of plummeting to the rain forest below, she tumbled back and landed on the broken tail of the vehicle, clinging for her life.

"Dani!" Mike yelled, standing up in his seat, looking past the captain at his sister for what he feared might be the last time.

"Take the wheel!" Captain Kevin leapt up. He leaned over the back of his seat and out over the fuselage toward Dani.

Mike jumped up onto his seat—facing backward—and grabbed the yoke.

Captain Kevin stretched out his arm.

Dani was still several feet away.

The captain cursed.

"Captain?" she whimpered.

Taking a deep breath and gritting his teeth, Captain Kevin pulled himself out of his compartment and onto the tail section, straddling it like a man on a horse.

Slowly, he inched toward her.

The plane bucked and Captain Kevin nearly toppled over the side.

"Hey, watch it!" he yelled back over his shoulder at Mike.

Mike, still standing in the passenger's seat, was flying blind with his fingers barely gripping the yoke.

"I'm trying!" he cried.

The metal beneath Dani shifted with a dangerous-sounding creak. The rest of the tail wasn't going to hold much longer.

"It's gonna break off," she cried.

"Eyes on me, Dani," said the captain. "Eyes on me."

He scooched and crawled farther along the spine of the

plane, inching toward her. The captain reached out again with one of his arms.

Dani stretched out to meet it.

Mike held his breath in anticipation.

They were still inches apart.

The back of the plane dropped another few inches. If the captain moved out any farther, it was not going to hold. Captain Kevin and Dani would fall to their doom and, without any tail at all, Mike and the rest of the plane would plummet down soon after them.

With one last heroic scooch, the captain lunged forward and grabbed Dani's hand in his own. She took it and lost hold of the plane. Dani slipped over the side, hanging precariously over the edge.

"Pull her in!" Mike yelled.

"She's heavier than she looks!" Captain Kevin cried.

"Then use both hands!" Mike screamed.

"I can't!"

"Why not?!"

The captain looked down over the side of the lurching plane. In one hand, he held the tiny hand of the little girl he had met only two days before. In his other hand, he held his future.

The jewel.

He couldn't possibly hold on to them both. If he held on to the jewel, he wouldn't be able to hoist Dani up, and soon, very soon, she would slip from his grasp. The only way to save her was to use both hands, meaning he had to let go of the only tangible thing he had to show for this adventure.

The captain released the jewel into the air and grabbed on to Dani with both hands.

Straining, grimacing, he pulled her up onto the shaking plane and eased her down into the driver's seat.

"Thanks," was all Dani could say. She was in shock.

"Thank you. Really," Mike added. "But it may not matter now. This plane is going down!"

CHAPTER 36
OKAY, THIS TIME THEY REALLY DO DIE

MIKE, DANI, AND CAPTAIN KEVIN were going to die.

Mike knew it for sure this time.

It wasn't the first time he'd had that thought. Truth be told, it wasn't the first time he'd had the thought *that morning*.

The banana he'd scarfed down earlier wasn't sitting well. His stomach was being "grumpy," as Dani would say. It was either the banana . . . or possibly the vertigo from plummeting out of the sky like a rock.

"This is it, Momo!" hollered Dani over the roar of the air ripping past them.

"Not if I can help it," shouted Captain Kevin as he wrestled with the controls. He flexed his arms and pulled with all his strength, ripping the entire yoke out of the dash.

"Nope. Can't help it. We're all gonna die."

Mike leapt up in his seat and grabbed Captain Kevin.

"Put it back. Put it back. Put it back!" Mike yelled. That banana took his open mouth as an invitation to try to crawl its way back to the freedom of the outside world. But Mike gulped and swallowed it back down.

The captain shrugged and tossed the yoke behind him like a gum wrapper.

Mike saw that all that was left of the steering column were some wires and a sheared pole that disappeared under the dash.

Somehow, things were getting worse.

Dani pointed and yelled something. Mike couldn't hear her, but they all could see what she was pointing at.

"*Roger*!" hollered Captain Kevin.

There, on the river below, was Captain Kevin's tour boat, still drifting along, just as they had left it. Impossible—and yet, there it was.

"How the heck is that thing still floating?" Mike asked.

"He's a tenacious one, he is. He's got more lives than an Amazonian spitting fish."

"How many lives do they have?" Dani asked.

"One," the captain said. "But he's got more than that."

The plane shook violently as they dropped toward the river.

Suddenly, the captain stuck his tongue out and made a noise like a startled river otter.

"What?" asked Dani.

"Idea!" said Captain Kevin, practically jumping up and down. "A bad one!"

He grabbed at the exposed wires and what was left of the sheared steering column and pulled. Mike felt the plane shift. It wasn't much, but it was something.

It began to level out. The river below stretched out like a long, brown-green landing strip that it clearly wasn't.

There would be no landing strip.

There would be no landing.

The plane was headed for the boat. They were going to crash right into it.

"We're gonna crash!" yelled Mike.

"We're gonna crash!" yelled Dani.

"You're right!" the captain yelled with bravado. "But where? That's the question!"

Mike and Dani clung to each other and shut their eyes. *At least we're together,* Mike thought.

Using every ounce of strength in his body, Captain Kevin pulled. The nose of the plane lifted slightly. They banked almost imperceptibly to the left, and true to everyone's prediction, they crashed.

The impact was tremendous, tearing the top half of the *Roger Oberholtzer* free and dragging the bottom half across the water like a speedboat.

Their bodies tumbled out and onto the deck like billiard balls. The once regurgitated banana in Mike's belly quickly followed suit.

In a stunt that was half brilliant and half stupid, Captain Kevin had landed the plummeting plane on his own limping, damaged ship.

Mike got up on wobbly legs and was shocked to see that the small cabin of the boat had been miraculously replaced by the plane's fuselage. It looked like the *Roger Oberholtzer* had actually eaten the biplane.

The three of them checked one another for broken bones, missing limbs, or any other visible trauma. The emotional scars would take decades to recover from, but other than Mike's leg, they were, more or less, fine.

"We're alive!" said Mike.

"Again!" shouted Dani.

"I'm home!" chimed in Captain Kevin, who dropped to his knees and kissed his boat. "*Roger*! I'm so glad to see you again."

He hugged the railing fiercely, then suddenly pulled back as if insulted.

"No, I'm not going to apologize. I had to use that explosive."

"Yeah, about that," Mike said, scratching his head. "You blew a hole in the bottom of a boat. How the heck is this thing still afloat?"

"Hey, you're a poet and you didn't even know it!" the captain said.

The boat shuddered in protest.

"Fine, fine. I'll go down and take a look," the captain sighed, trudging down below to look at the damage.

Ten seconds later, he was back on deck, holding his nose with an expression of revulsion.

"Do not go down there."

"What is it?" Dani asked.

"What's got four legs, a tail, and stinks to high heaven?" the captain said with distaste. "Lesson for the day: a rotting caiman does not a pleasant smell make."

"*Ewwww.*" Dani's face scrunched up in disgust.

"Apparently, he tried to fit through the hole and was a bit too tubby," Captain Kevin noted. "Plugged the leak, though!"

"Awww, poor thing." Dani frowned.

"Poor thing?" Mike balked. "It was trying to eat us!"

"It's his nature," Dani explained gently. "It's the circle of life."

Mike was about to inform her that her cartoon philosophy wasn't nearly as heartwarming when she was the meal, but a strange rumbling sound in the distance demanded his attention.

Something wasn't right. Mike tasted banana in his throat again.

Funny thing about waterfalls: you can hear them *before* you see them. And Mike could hear one roaring downriver.

"Waterfall!" he shouted.

"What do we do?" Dani asked, turning to Captain Kevin.

The captain threw up his hands.

"I don't know! I thought we were goners on that plane," he confessed. "I didn't expect us to make it *this* far! Every moment since then has been a gift!"

Mike cursed his luck. Once again, they were going to die.

CHAPTER 37
A BAD IDEA

"**W**E HAVE TO STOP THE BOAT," Mike said as the *Roger Oberholtzer* picked up speed, careening toward the falls. "Quick. Drop the anchor!"

"We don't have an anchor," the captain said. "It's a cooler, remember?"

Dani turned to Captain Kevin and hugged his waist as tight as a girdle. "I could really use a joke right about now."

"Really?" he said. "You think *this* is scarier than when we were about to crash a plane?"

"I'm just a kid!" Dani shot back. "I can't help what scares me!"

Captain Kevin stuck out his chin defiantly, roping Dani under one arm and pulling Mike close with the other.

"Well, at least you two will die comforted by the fact that I was the best thing that ever happened to you."

"You are not!" hollered Mike, raising his voice over the rumble of the waterfall.

"You're right," agreed Captain Kevin. "I was the best thing that ever happened to *me*." Mike broke out of Captain Kevin's embrace.

"We need your help, not your quitting hugs of death!"

Mike realized that, once again, he couldn't rely on the captain to get them out of this. He scanned the boat, the plane, and the river, looking everywhere at everything as his mind raced to find a way out of this. The thoughts came fast and furious.

Steer the ship to the shore. Break up on rocks. All die.

Lasso a hanging branch. Line breaks. Over the falls. All die.

Jump overboard and swim. Seriously? Are you kidding? All die.

He thought his head was going to explode. Mike purposely banged it against the belly of the plane. He was thinking too much. Maybe that was his biggest problem.

This wasn't a problem to solve. This was an adventure to seize. And adventures demanded risks.

He forced himself to stop thinking and just act.

"Forget common sense," he said, a small incongruous smile appearing on his face.

Suddenly, Mike was limping as quickly as he could around the small tour boat, collecting rope and jungle vines—and even old flags that were tucked into holes in the deck.

"Help me!" said Mike. "I've got a really bad idea!"

Mike tied what was left of the plane's landing gear to the deck of the boat.

A hundred yards in front of them, the river ended abruptly.

There was only mist and the lionlike roar of the waterfall growing louder.

"Momo," said Captain Kevin. "Are you doing what I think you're doing?"

"I know. It's terrible," said Mike. "But it's either go with the bad idea or the death hugs."

"Or both," added Captain Kevin.

"Talking is not as helpful as tying!" barked Mike.

"Uhhhh, Momo," Dani said. "Family meeting."

"No time," Mike yelled. "We have to tie this down, now!"

"We're tying the plane to the boat so that it doesn't fall, it . . . *flies?*" Dani was shocked. "That is so, well, so *Captain Kevin-y.*"

"Bad idea?" asked Mike.

"The worst!" Dani grinned. She ran up and hugged her brother around the neck, then grabbed the line of vines out of his hands and wrapped the nearest strut to the boat deck.

The three of them worked as fast as they could, knowing that every second they were drawing closer to where the river ended and death began.

"There's no way this is going to work," mumbled Mike to himself.

"You're right . . ." said Captain Kevin.

"You're not supposed to say that!" Mike climbed up into the plane. "You're supposed to say, 'Of course it will work,' or 'I believe in you.'"

The captain paused for a moment, then squinted up at Mike.

"You want me to *lie*?"

Mike sighed and climbed into the pilot's seat, his nerves frayed like an old sweater that was about to go over a waterfall. He grabbed the handfuls of wire with one hand and the last remaining bits of the yoke with the other, just as Captain Kevin had done. The captain and Dani crawled into the other seat.

Mike snuck a look out in front of them, where the river vanished.

Dani gave her brother a worried look.

He ruffled her hair and gave her a smile, before quoting the captain back to her.

"I got this," he said.

It was now or never. Or both.

His stomach rumbled nervously, and despite the fear racing through his every nerve, he burped.

It smelled like bananas.

CHAPTER 38
YOU GOTTA BE KIDDING ME!

IN MOST ADVENTURES, riding a half boat, half plane over the brink of a waterfall would be enough.

The participants could justifiably say that they had faced the danger, been through the wringer, and qualified themselves as adventurers. Adding any more peril on top of that would be overkill.

Unbelievable.

Ridiculous.

Then a vengeful scream was heard over the roaring of the tumbling water.

The temple monster was back.

"Aw, come on," Mike groaned, hitting the console with frustration. "Give me a break."

The towering creature crashed through the jungle, tearing through trees like blades of grass beneath its feet.

"Go! Go! Go!" yelled Captain Kevin.

"You want me to go *faster* over the waterfall?" Mike asked.

The giant rock thing slammed one colossal foot into the river, sending tidal waves of water up onto the shore.

"What do you want from me?" the captain screamed at the Goliath. "I don't have any of your stupid jewels! Go away!"

"Yeah," Dani said, her voice trembling. "Now I think he's just mad."

An enormous stone hand reached out, dwarfing the boat.

"He's going to crush us!" Dani cried.

"Hang on!" Mike yelled, pulling hard on the guts of the controls as the boat tipped forward. "Time to take a leap!"

Mike closed his eyes, and they went over the edge.

Behind them, the hulking temple creature lunged.

In front of them, there was only mist and sky.

The water roared.

The temple howled.

The passengers screamed.

The *Roger Oberholtzer* plummeted over the falls and into oblivion.

Captain Kevin clung to Dani like a frightened child.

And then the bizarre boat-plane bad-idea hybrid caught the air.

It shuddered as the wind under its wings lifted the "vehicle" away from the falls and into the sky. They were, for lack of a better word, *fall*-flying.

And a shadow fell over them.

The temple monster had stumbled at the falls, its last attempt to grab them carrying it over the edge. It plummeted toward them and the hard rocky ground below.

"It's gonna crush us!" squealed the captain, who shut his eyes tight.

"No way! I'm not getting stuck between a rock monster and a hard place," Mike yelled.

"Hey! Another joke," Captain Kevin said, pleased.

Mike pulled back on the yoke with everything he had and felt the boat-plane shudder beneath him as it strained to lift higher into the air.

The titanic monster hurtled down after them.

The ground was rushing up.

The plane was about to rip apart.

Mike urged the boat-plane a few more feet away from the falls.

The hulking creature passed inches from the vehicle's stern, then plummeted helplessly toward the rocks below.

Its monumental body shattered on impact, like a stone castle dropped out of the sky. Pieces of debris flew in every direction and a large stone clipped the wing of the boat-plane.

"Hang on," Mike yelled again. "This is gonna be rough."

He braced himself and gritted his teeth as the boat-plane slammed down onto the water, cracking like a pistachio and losing large pieces that appeared vital to the vehicle's integrity.

The undulating current further shook and rattled the boat in the aftermath of the waterfall, tossing the occupants back to the deck. But slowly, gradually, the water settled down and the boat drifted gently down the Amazon once again.

They all stared at one another in disbelief for a moment— and then Mike exploded.

"Woo-hoo!" he whooped into the air. "That was awesome! Did you see that? Better than a freakin' roller coaster!"

"Who are you and what have you done with my brother?" Dani laughed. She squeezed him tight, like an anaconda. "You did it, Momo. You took a risk! And look! We survived. And we had an adventure!"

"I believe it now. I believe in adventure. It still exists!" Mike laughed. "We did it. And I'll never do it again!"

He didn't really mean the last part. Over the last two days, Mike had acquired something of a taste for adventure.

"We're gonna have to call you Momo the Waterfall Wizard," the captain said, smiling, before ruffling Dani's hair. "And you Bermuda Betty."

"And don't forget this guy." Mike grinned, slapping the railing. "You did it, Mr. *Oberholtzer*!"

Captain Kevin looked at the kids with something bordering on genuine affection.

"You can call him *Roger*. You've earned it," replied the captain.

Then he cleared his throat and adjusted his hat, hiding his eyes beneath its brim.

"You're both officially Shipwreckers now," he added.

Mike felt like he'd just been knighted. The idea of a "Shipwrecker" had seemed so idiotic to him at the start of all this. But now, it really felt like a badge of honor, one he would wear proudly.

Captain Kevin then quickly snapped to attention, saluting Mike.

Mike smiled and gave the captain a salute in return.

Captain Kevin turned to salute Dani as well. She grinned and embraced him in an unrelenting bear hug. He hugged her back.

After the inevitable awkward silence that always follows an outburst of affection, the captain cleared his throat again and took the wheel of his slowly deteriorating vessel.

Mike grinned. Wet, beaten, and bedraggled atop a boat-plane hybrid, the three of them must have made quite a sight: Bermuda Betty, Momo the Waterfall Wizard, and Captain Kevin Adventureson, three oddballs thrown together by fate, like something out of one of his books. Luckily, this was a book with a happily ever after.

Standing on the deck with the two kids still beside him, the captain appeared to have a revelation.

"Maybe, in some way I don't fully understand, I needed you kids," admitted Captain Kevin. "Sure, you were irritating, particularly the boy one, but you were both brighter than you looked, and in a way, you helped steer me in the right direction. And considering my own internal compass has been broken for years, that might be something valuable." He shrugged. "Or maybe my blood sugar is low and I need to eat something."

Mike decided to take it as a compliment.

As the remains of the *Roger Oberholtzer* sailed back down the river, Captain Kevin made one more announcement: "If you'll look to your left, you'll see the Amazon tributary that leads back to the village where your parents are waiting for you."

Then he hesitated, a mischievous gleam in his eye as he turned the ship sharply to the right.

"But first, I just gotta see a guy about a treasure chest; this is just a little detour. Should be a few hours. Tops. Deal?"

Dani looked to her brother with a gleam in her eye.

"Deal!" shouted Dani.

Mike felt his heart drop into his stomach.

"What?!"

FROM THE JOURNAL OF CAPTAIN
KEVIN ADVENTURESON

I know a lot of you look up to me . . . and to be honest, I don't blame you.

I am not just a role model. I'm also a bona fide font of knowledge and useful information.

But if I had to leave you with one last thought—in addition to all the other amazing thoughts I've already left you with—it would be this: Don't leave any loose ends.

Here's the thing. So many adventurers, explorers, spelunkers, and ruggedly handsome archaeologists make it 99 percent of the way to the end of their quest and then drop the ball on the last play.

So, when you've found the treasure . . . or rescued the hostage . . . or evaded the authorities, and you think you're home free, stop! Look around. What have you forgotten about? Chances are you've left a stick of dynamite burning, or forgotten to tighten your trusty peg leg, or neglected to pay off the guy who is supposed to be your alibi. And that's when the monkey doo hits the fan.

But if you're like me, you'll pay attention to detail

and stay on the job until everything, EVERYTHING,
is taken care of, put to bed, read a bedtime story,
and rocked to sleep.

No loose ends!

If I had learned that lesson a little earlier, I might
still have my pinky toes.

CHAPTER 39
FROM THE ASHES

THE FURIOUS WATER at the base of the waterfall twisted and tumbled, churning the remains of the temple over and over, breaking it down and down and down, its treasures sinking to the bottom of the Amazon.

Suddenly, there was a terrible cry, something not quite human, raging at the sky.

Birds at the shore took flight for safer harbor as a hand burst from beneath the foam.

Rising up from the wreckage of the stone monster, a twisted, skinless arm reached out, clawing at the air.

It was raw and desiccated as if cursed by some horrible disease.

It was a woman's arm . . . or at least it had been.

Somehow, someone inside the temple had survived the fall.

She was alive.

And she was screaming.

Screaming a man's name.

"Captaaain Keviiiiin!"

THE END

ACKNOWLEDGMENTS

THANKS FIRST AND FOREMOST to our incredible editor, Brittany Rubiano, for her unwavering support of *Shipwreckers*. She believed in it long before anyone else did and rallied, pushed, advocated, and badgered on our behalf for nearly two years until it became real. She also appreciates bad puns and probably likes Captain Kevin more than we do.

Thanks to Nachie Marsham, Kieran Viola, Megan Logan, and all the folks at Disney Press and Disney-Hyperion for all their assistance. We'd also like to thank them in advance for all the lobbying we *hope* they'll be doing for *Shipwreckers 2: Bermuda Triangle Doom Cruise of Doom* and *Shipwreckers 3: How Are These Kids Still Alive?*

Extra-special thanks to Brian Ajhar for his incredible cover and illustrations, and for bringing our characters to life!

We want to thank our reps, Julie Kane-Ritsch at Gotham Group and Deborah Warren at East West Literary Agency; so we *will* thank them for their support, enthusiasm, and frequent hand-holding. We're high-maintenance, but we're worth it.

And finally, we'd like to thank our wives, Amanda and Cindy, for their encouragement and support, because as any married man will tell you, you're an idiot if you don't thank your wife.

For more information about the authors, you can check out Scott Peterson at www.flagrantproductions.net and Joshua Pruett at www.joshuapruett.com.

So, get out there and take some risks. Like Captain Kevin said, "Nothing adventured, nothing *adgained*!"